Quiet Nights

💀

ETERNAL REST
BED AND BREAKFAST

PARANORMAL COZY MYSTERIES

BETH DOLGNER

Quiet Nights
Eternal Rest Bed and Breakfast Book Seven
© 2022 Beth Dolgner

All rights reserved. No portion of this book may be reproduced in any form without permission from the publisher, except as permitted by U.S. copyright law.

ISBN: 978-1-958587-03-4

Quiet Nights is a work of fiction. Names, characters, places, and incidents either are the products of the author's imagination or are used fictitiously. Any resemblance to actual persons, living or dead, businesses, companies, events, or locales is entirely coincidental.

Published by Redglare Press
Cover by Dark Mojo Designs
Print Formatting by The Madd Formatter

https://bethdolgner.com

1

I can do this. I can do this. I can do this.

Emily took in a deep breath as she tried to drown out the noise in the room. The other people seated around the dining room table were trying to be quiet, but even the sounds of their breathing seemed to blare in Emily's ears. She heard a creak as someone shifted in their chair.

"I am trying to contact the ghosts of Eternal Rest," Emily said quietly. "Mrs. Thompson, Kelly, Grandma Gray: are any of you there? If so, can you please give us a sign of your presence?"

Emily cracked one eye open and instantly realized it was a mistake. Instead of seeing any evidence of paranormal activity, she saw only eight pairs of eyes directed eagerly toward her, all shining in the light of the purple seven-day candle that sat in the middle of the table.

"Focus," Sage said. Emily was seated at the head of the table, and Sage was immediately to her right. Sage leaned forward and put a comforting hand on Emily's arm. She gave a reassuring squeeze, then left her hand there. "Feel my energy flowing to you. Use it. Use Reed's."

Emily closed her eyes again. She pictured her former assistant in her mind, recalling one of their many conversations in that very room. It had been almost a year since Mrs. Thompson had died, and her ghost had been a welcome resident at Eternal Rest Bed and Breakfast ever since. Emily focused on the memory of Mrs. Thompson's thin hands wrapped around a coffee cup, her eyes shining merrily in her wrinkled face. "Mrs. Thompson, we would love to visit with you," Emily said. "Can you please knock on the wall to let us know if you're here with us?"

A knock sounded firmly on the wall to Emily's left.

Emily heard a few excited gasps from her guests, and Sage gave her arm another squeeze.

Emily grinned. "Thank you, Mrs. Thompson! We're so glad you're here. You know the drill: we'll ask you yes or no questions, and you can knock once for yes, and twice for no. Do you understand?"

Knock.

"We have new guests for you to meet, though I believe you already met Joe and Alana. Was that you who moved their suitcase from the bed into the closet?"

Knock.

"That was so nice of you to help, Mrs. Thompson." Emily paused for a moment to appreciate how communicative Mrs. Thompson was being. Emily had been talking to the ghosts of Eternal Rest for the past week as she cleaned and made up the guest rooms, begging for their cooperation.

It should have been Sage leading the séance. Since Emily had started offering the Spirited Saturday Night package at Eternal Rest, it had been Sage sitting at the head of the table, chatting easily with the house's resident ghosts as well as any other spirits who wanted to talk with the guests.

Emily wouldn't be able to channel messages from her guests' deceased loved ones, like Sage could, but at least Mrs. Thompson and Kelly should be easy for Emily to communicate with since she did so on a regular basis. She kept reminding herself that, this time, the only difference was that she had an audience for the conversations.

"Mrs. Thompson," Emily began. Before she could finish, she heard several loud knocks on the wall. "Mrs. Thompson, was that you?"

There was no answer.

"Mrs. Thompson, are you still there?" Now Emily's eyes were open as she glanced around the room. She felt a chill wash over her.

Has the energy in the room changed, or am I just scaring myself?

"The energy has shifted," Reed said. He was sitting next to Sage, and his dark-brown eyes fixed on Emily. "It's okay. We're here with you."

Emily wanted to ask Reed if he had been reading her mind, but instead, she said, "Everyone, please close your eyes. I'm going to ask Kelly Stern, the ghost of a seventeen-year-old girl who was murdered in the cemetery next door, to tell us what's going on. She only writes messages if no one is looking." Once everyone complied, Emily closed her own eyes again. "Kelly, can you tell us why the room feels different suddenly? Did Mrs. Thompson leave?"

As Emily counted out the seconds, wanting to give Kelly at least a minute to respond, she silently pleaded that Kelly would write in her usual big, swooping handwriting that the room felt different because Scott had decided to join them. Emily could even picture the smiley face Kelly would draw at the end of her sentence. As much as Emily wanted her late husband's ghost to be with them, though, she knew the goose bumps breaking out on her arms weren't from a loving spirit.

"Kelly, is there another ghost here?" Emily heard her voice shaking, and she felt a wave of nervousness. With a start, she realized the feeling wasn't coming from herself but rather her guests. She was picking up on their emotions.

In any other situation, Emily would have celebrated such progress in her burgeoning psychic abilities. At the moment, though, she just wanted to know what was going on.

After more than a minute had passed, Emily rose to look at the paper she always left sitting on the sideboard. She couldn't tell in the dim light whether there was writing on it, but she did notice the pen, which she had left sitting on top of the paper, was now on top of the stack of plates next to it.

Emily had only taken one step toward the sideboard when a concussion ripped through the room. Even as Emily heard the bang, the windows rattled and the candle flame wavered, then went out. Instinctively, Emily covered her head with her hands as the house shuddered around her.

In the silence that followed, Emily asked anxiously, "Is everyone okay?"

"Yeah, I think we're fine," one of her guests said in a wavering voice. Emily thought it was Steven Bates, who had come to Eternal Rest with his twenty-four-year-old daughter for a fun weekend of looking for ghosts.

So much for fun, Emily thought wryly.

The chandelier overhead suddenly blazed, and Emily looked up to see Reed standing by the door, his hand still on the light switch. Emily was relieved to realize Steven had been right. Not only were her guests fine, but she couldn't see any damage to the room around them.

"What was that?" Alana was looking at Emily with a panicked expression. She and Joe had been delighted when they discovered the ghost of Mrs. Thompson had moved their luggage. That, Emily had to remind herself, was a lot less frightening than what had sounded like a sonic boom.

"I don't know what caused that," Emily said honestly. "Let's see if Kelly has any insight."

Emily squeezed between her guests' chairs and the sideboard so she could grab the sheet of paper. As she brought it toward her, she could see Kelly's handwriting was small, and she felt her heart sink. Kelly only wrote that way when she was scared or upset.

It's the scary ghost, Kelly had written. *The one that you think killed Scott.*

Emily wasn't really surprised; after the way the room had felt and the sudden explosion of paranormal activity, she didn't know what else it could have been.

Emily turned her head toward the ceiling. "Kelly, I know you're all scared, but please help keep Scott safe."

"What did she write?" Alana asked. "And who's Scott?"

Emily glanced at Sage, who made a "go ahead" motion with her hand and said, "I think I know what you're about to say, and your guests should know what's going on."

Haltingly, Emily told them about Scott's car crash nearly three years before, and how she suspected it had been caused by some kind of dark entity. "It's continued following his spirit since then, keeping him drained of energy so he couldn't even come home. We don't know why," Emily said. "It was only three weeks ago that Scott was able to come through a powerful psychic barrier that surrounds this town, but he's been too weak to communicate with me since then."

"I'm sorry, Em," Sage said sadly. "I felt it when Scott came through that doorway the witches made in the barrier, but I didn't sense that the entity had followed him."

"We knew it was a risk bringing him home," Emily said.

Tyler and Dominique, a couple who had started the weekend saying they were skeptics, had been sitting silently, their arms around each other. Tyler glanced at his wife, then said, "This is the first thing we've experienced this weekend.

Maybe it only happened because we were sitting here inviting ghosts to come visit us. I mean, we were literally asking for it."

Well, I guess they aren't skeptics anymore.

"I was actually calling out to Mrs. Thompson and Kelly," Emily said, unable to keep a slightly defensive tone out of her voice. "Sage and I have learned the hard way that if the dark entity wants to show up, it will. It doesn't wait for an invitation."

"Still," Tyler said, rising, "I don't think we want to wait around for something else to happen. We're going to bed." Dominique followed Tyler silently out of the room, clinging tightly to his hand. Emily hated seeing her guests unhappy, but she couldn't blame them for wanting to get as far from the entity as possible.

Once Dominque had shut the door behind her, Steven turned his attention to Emily. He had keen hazel eyes and dark, bushy eyebrows that were constantly quirked, making it look like he was skeptical of anything anyone said to him. "So, your late husband's spirit is here, but he's weak? How does a ghost recover its energy?"

Emily nodded toward Sage. "Our resident psychic medium can answer that for you," she said.

Steven's daughter, Rylee, frowned, her dark-red lipstick amplifying her expression. "I thought you were the medium, Emily."

"Well, I'm learning," Emily said. "As you can see, I didn't do a great job tonight."

"I used to be a psychic medium," Sage said bitterly. "I lost all my abilities."

"For now," Reed broke in. "You'll recover them."

"How did you lose your abilities?" Rylee's gray eyes were wide under her black bangs.

Sage swept a hand around the table. "All of this. Getting Scott through the barrier, facing that entity a couple times, and the unbelievable number of ghosts who came into Oak Hill before the barrier's strength was restored. It exhausted me physically, and then it exhausted me psychically."

Rylee sat back, her eyes darting around the room nervously.

"Don't worry, you're not in danger," Sage said. "My energy is recovering, and, like Reed said, my mediumship abilities will, too. Hopefully. He and I are just here tonight to lend moral support to Emily. It's her first time leading the séance on one of these weekends."

"You did great," Alana said. "However, Joe and I are going to bed, too. I don't think I could handle anything more exciting than what just happened."

Emily wished them a good night as they left. She noticed Steven and Rylee showed no interest in leaving, and she said apologetically, "I think we're done for the night. That was the shortest séance we've ever had here, but it was definitely the wildest."

Rylee looked relieved, but Steven seemed disappointed. "We'll see you at breakfast, then," he said. "Alana is right: you did a great job tonight."

Emily was still holding Kelly's note, and she put it down with a sigh as the last of her guests filed out of the room. "Would either of you like a glass of wine?" she asked Reed and Sage.

"I'll get it," Reed said. "You go sit in the parlor and relax."

Emily and Sage were soon settled onto the Victorian sofa in the parlor, which was across the hall from the dining room. "I appreciate you and Reed coming to support me tonight," Emily said. "I'm surprised Trevor didn't come, too."

"I invited him, but he said he already had plans," Sage

said, leaning her head back against the sofa. "He's taking someone out for dinner tonight."

Emily jerked her head toward Sage, then saw her best friend had her eyes closed. She asked herself why the news that Trevor Williams had a date had sent a jolt through her. *He should be here, with me,* Emily thought, then caught herself. *No, he's been here for me a lot lately. He deserves to go out and have some fun. I'm being selfish.*

That's all it is. Right?

Realizing she hadn't responded to Sage, Emily simply said, "Oh."

Reed came into the parlor, balancing a bottle of wine and three glasses on a tray. "We have earned this tonight," he said as he put the tray on the coffee table in front of the sofa.

No sooner had Reed spoken than there was another booming noise, followed by the shriek of shattering glass.

Instead of cringing like she had earlier, Emily leapt up from the couch, already looking at the parlor windows to see if any of them were broken. Sage seemed to have shrunk into the couch, her fingers clutching the edge of the cushion.

"Is this what it's like for normal people to experience paranormal activity?" she asked. "This is awful! I know something strange is going on, but I can't sense who or what is causing it. Oh, I hate this!"

"Reed, stay with Sage," Emily ordered. Her anger that the entity was destroying things in her house was overriding her fear at the moment. Since the parlor appeared untouched, Emily rushed into the dining room, but everything there was in place.

Emily hurried down the hallway and stopped short in front of the kitchen doorway. She immediately knew that was where the sound of shattering glass had come from. Earlier, she had put dirty glasses next to the sink, planning to move them to the dishwasher later. Every single one of them had been swept off the counter, and they lay in a broken heap on the floor. Glass shards had exploded outward from the impact, and the entire kitchen floor twinkled as the tiny pieces caught the light.

"What do you want?" Emily shouted at the empty

kitchen. She could feel the muscles in her chest tightening, and she resisted the urge to scream out her frustration. After everything they had been through, Scott still wasn't safe.

There were two loud knocks on the wall next to the kitchen door.

"Mrs. Thompson?"

Knock.

"Are you okay?"

Five knocks sounded slowly. During the séance, Mrs. Thompson's final knocks had seemed urgent, but these were soft and measured.

"Are you telling me to calm down?"

Knock.

"I know that's good advice, Mrs. Thompson. I'm just so ready to help Scott find peace, and this thing isn't letting that happen. I want to scream at it and ask it what it wants."

This time, the knocks came at a rapid pace before finally tapering off.

Emily pictured Mrs. Thompson during one of their many chats, back when she had been Emily's assistant. The woman had always been calm and kind, and she had once told Emily that the key to a good life was to think before acting.

Emily felt a small smile at the corners of her mouth as she heard Mrs. Thompson's voice in her head, doling out advice. "Are you telling me not to provoke the entity?" she asked.

Knock.

"Good advice, as always. I'm just scared and upset and angry, and about a hundred other feelings. More than anything, I just want Scott to be okay. If this entity is still following him, then it's no wonder he can't communicate with us. I bet it's still draining his energy."

When the ghost of Mrs. Thompson knocked again, it had a soft, almost sympathetic tone.

Emily heard footsteps in the hallway behind her, and she turned, putting out a warning hand. "Watch out, there's a ton of broken glass." She had expected to see Reed and Sage, but instead, it was Steven and Rylee. "I'm sorry about the noise, both from me and the entity," Emily said.

"It's okay," Rylee said quickly. "After what you told us about it and what it's doing to your husband's spirit, I totally get it. I would be shouting, too."

"Emily," Reed called. Emily looked up and saw him near the foot of the stairs. "I'm going to reassure your other guests that everything is okay. They're up on the landing."

"Thanks." Emily doubted everything was okay, but there was no reason to say that in front of her guests.

Steven cleared his throat and glanced at Rylee. "I, uh, think it's time we had a talk with you, Emily," he said.

Emily frowned. "About what?"

"Rylee isn't my daughter, and we're not really on a father-daughter trip."

Ew, she's so much younger than him.

"I'm the producer of a new documentary TV series, and Rylee is part of the talent. She's a psychic medium, too."

Oh, good. I don't have to be weirded out by their relationship.

Rylee nodded. "The real star of the show is Tessa Valentine."

Emily heard a snort behind Steven and Rylee. All she could see was the top of Sage's spiked pink hair, but she could just picture the look of contempt on her face. "Do you know her, Sage?" Emily asked.

Steven and Rylee moved so they could peer at Sage. She stood with her arms crossed. "I used to know her,"

Sage said pointedly. "We were never friends, but we used to attend some of the same events."

"She's one of the most popular and successful psychic mediums in the country," Steven said. "All of her books have been bestsellers, and on her last tour, every stop was sold out."

"She's a hack," Sage spat.

Rylee remained silent, but Emily noticed how uncomfortable she looked. Her head bent downward, but she kept looking from Steven to Sage under her eyelids.

"Her track record says otherwise," Steven countered.

Sage was opening her mouth to retort when Emily cut her off. "I've heard of Tessa, too, of course," she said hastily, "though I've never met her."

"Hopefully you'll get to form your own *accurate* opinion of her soon," Steven said, returning his attention to Emily. "We're in Oak Hill this week, filming an episode of the show, and Eternal Rest came to our attention during our research. Rylee and I stayed here, posing as a father and daughter, to check out the claims. Rylee has sensed enough to know your hauntings are legitimate, so we're interested in including your B and B in the episode. Tessa will come here to communicate with your ghosts, and of course, we'll work in the history of the place."

Behind Steven, Sage was shaking her head wildly, a slightly horrified look on her face.

"I'll consider it," Emily said carefully. While the publicity might be great for business, Emily wanted to know more about Tessa—and why Sage so strongly disliked her—before committing to anything. She also found Steven and Rylee's deception off-putting. If they were scouting out Eternal Rest for a TV show, then why hadn't they just been honest about it in the first place?

"Consider fast," Steven said, smiling. "We're filming at our first Oak Hill location on Monday. We had planned to film at an old hotel outside of town on Wednesday, but we're getting reports that it's no longer haunted."

Sage laughed. "Let me guess: Mountain View Manor? Emily already helped those ghosts and got them to cross over."

Steven smiled at Emily, though it looked more cunning than friendly. "All the more reason for you to let us film here instead," he said. "So, does Wednesday work for you?"

"Like I said," Emily answered, "I'll consider it."

"Good, good. We'll head back to bed. Let's hope it's a peaceful night for all of us." Steven nodded at Emily, then turned and headed for the stairway, Rylee following silently in his wake. He glanced darkly at Sage as he passed her.

As soon as they had retreated upstairs, Emily leaned toward Sage and whispered, "Why don't you like Tessa? Do you really think she's a hack?"

Sage pursed her lips. "I would need a couple glasses of wine before going down that road," she said sourly. "Unfortunately, we have a mess to clean up first. You grab the broom, and I'll get a trash bag."

Cleaning up the broken glass took a while, since shards had scattered all the way to the other side of the kitchen. There were even a few pieces in the hallway, which Emily only noticed when they crunched under her shoes. Reed pitched in after he came back downstairs, saying the rest of Emily's guests had calmed down sufficiently to go to bed. "But I think it's a good thing they're all checking out tomorrow," he added. "Otherwise, Tyler and Dominique would probably be heading home early and asking for a refund."

"It's bad enough this entity is hurting Scott, but now it's going to hurt my business, too," Emily grumbled. "I can just picture the online reviews from this weekend.

Maybe I should let them film that show here to get a little positive publicity."

"Show?" Reed asked.

Emily quickly filled him in as Sage inserted derogatory comments about Tessa Valentine. When she was done, Reed just chuckled. "I knew there was something off about those two. They didn't strike me as a father and daughter."

"And yet you claim not to be a psychic," Emily teased.

Reed shrugged. "I'm just a good observer of people."

Finally, the broken glass was cleaned up, and the kitchen floor was mopped. Sage sighed. "I need to go home. My energy has improved a lot in the past few weeks, but I'm not fully recovered. I'll have to take a rain check on the wine."

Even though Sage's psychic abilities had been exhausted, she had begun to recover some of her physical energy. Emily felt exhausted, too. The discovery that the dark entity had followed Scott through the barrier had left her feeling shaken and vulnerable.

"Thanks for the help tonight, both of you," Emily said. "I'll ask Kelly and Mrs. Thompson to keep me posted on whatever is going on here." Emily walked her friends to the front door, then hugged both of them tightly before saying good night.

With a weary sigh, Emily returned to the kitchen. The floor was mostly dry, and she walked carefully to the coffee maker to get it prepped for the next morning. When that was done, she retreated into her bedroom. Normally, it felt like a refuge from the world, but knowing the entity was in the house only made her room seem like some sort of trap.

Emily took off her necklace, which had a graceful pendant in the shape of the letter *E*. It had been a gift from Scott. As she put it in her jewelry box, Emily noticed the sheet of paper sitting next to it on the dresser had writing on it. Kelly's handwriting wasn't her usual large size, but at least it wasn't small and timid, either.

The scary thing isn't here right now.

Below that, Kelly had written another line that made Emily gasp.

He's ready to talk.

Emily looked around her bedroom, almost expecting to see Scott standing there. She felt a pang of disappointment when she didn't see him, and she had to remind herself that he was just a ghost. She sat on the edge of her bed and closed her eyes. "Scott? Are you there?"

When there was no response, she called, "You can knock on the walls like Mrs. Thompson, or write a note, like Kelly. They can help you do those things, I'm sure."

Still, nothing happened. Emily even opened her eyes and looked at the paper on her dresser, but there was no new writing on it.

Emily sighed. "Mrs. Thompson, are you there?"

Knock.

"Can you and Kelly please help Scott communicate? Kelly says he's ready, but he seems to be having a hard time."

Knock.

Emily tried to reach out with her mind, like Sage had instructed her to do when she first began developing the ability to interact with ghosts. She didn't know how many minutes passed as she focused on sensing the room around her, but eventually, Emily felt a change. The air in front of her felt charged, like it was vibrating with electricity.

"Scott, is that you?" Emily held her breath. What she was sensing didn't make her feel chilled, like the dark entity did.

There was a knock on the wall, and Emily took it as Mrs. Thompson's confirmation that it was, indeed, Scott standing in front of her.

"Scott, you can give yes or no answers for Mrs. Thompson to pass along, or you can give me more detailed answers by asking Kelly to write them. Do you understand?"

A knock confirmed that Scott understood the plan. "You've been home for three weeks now. Have you recovered some of your energy?"

There was no response from Mrs. Thompson, so after a few minutes, Emily got up and checked the paper on her dresser.

Yes, but I've been hiding. Didn't want to bring something so dark home to you. I think she was scared to come inside because of your ghosts, but she's getting impatient.

Emily's eyebrows knit together. "She?"

Before Emily could ask Scott to elaborate, there was a loud scream from somewhere above Emily's head, followed by the sound of running feet.

3

As Emily ran into the hallway, she could hear footsteps pounding down the stairs. Soon, Rylee appeared ahead of her. "I think it's after me! That malevolent spirit is trying to hurt me!"

Emily stopped and stared hard at Rylee, looking for any signs she was injured. Rylee had changed into a tank top and pajama pants, and Emily couldn't see any cuts or bruises on her pale arms. "What did it do to you?" Emily asked.

"Come upstairs and see," Rylee said in between deep gulps of air.

Emily followed Rylee up the stairs, and she wasn't surprised when she reached the second-floor landing and found all of her guests gathered there, looking terrified. Rylee went straight to her room. She had left the door standing wide open, and before they reached it, Emily could already see that the floor was littered with something.

Rylee stepped aside and made a sweeping motion with her hand, and Emily edged past her to survey the room. The floor was covered in leaves and petals: the fresh flowers Emily had put in a vase on the dresser had been completely ripped apart. The sheets and pillows had been yanked off the bed, and it looked as if every single item in

Rylee's suitcase had been taken out and piled behind the antique rocking chair that sat in one corner.

At least, Emily thought, *nothing is broken.*

"Did you see this happen?" Emily asked.

Rylee shook her head. "No, I was in the bathroom, getting ready for bed. When I came out, I found it like this."

"Did you hear anything strange while it was going on?"

Again, Rylee shook her head.

Emily had felt panic when Rylee screamed, then claimed the entity had tried to hurt her. However, as she surveyed the chaotic guest room, Emily felt a sense of calm settle over her. Rylee hadn't even been in the room when this had happened, which meant whatever had caused it hadn't been trying to hurt her. Not only that, but the only actual damage done was to the flowers. Emily had to wonder if the dark entity was even responsible for the mess, or if it had been some other ghost or paranormal phenomenon. Kelly had written, *The scary thing isn't here right now*, and Emily had taken that to mean it wasn't in the house at all. Emily supposed Kelly could have meant it simply wasn't in Emily's bedroom with them, but even still, given the entity's past behavior, unmaking a bed and moving clothing seemed rather mild.

Emily glanced at Rylee, whose chest was still heaving, then noticed Steven was standing in the doorway, his mouth agape. "Don't touch anything," he said firmly. "I'm going to get my video camera. Rylee, go put on a bit of makeup so we can film your reaction to this." He spun around and disappeared, and Emily could have sworn he had a bounce in his step.

Maybe Rylee faked this whole thing for the TV show.

As Emily watched Rylee nod and retreat into the bathroom, she realized that thought might be entirely accurate. If Rylee had done this herself, she might have been careful not to do any irreparable damage. After the dark entity had broken the glasses in the kitchen, it didn't make sense that it would wreck a bedroom and not even smash the lamp on the nightstand or shatter the vase the flowers had been in.

Still, Emily didn't want to outright accuse a guest of faking a haunting, especially when her other guests were all crowded in the hallway. Instead, she turned to all of them and said, "I know seeing her room like this startled Rylee, but no real harm has been done, to her or the room. It looks like a ghost might have been trying to get her attention, but that's all."

"What if it trashes our room next?" Joe asked, his gaze going past Emily and into the room.

Steven returned before Emily could answer, elbowing his way past the other guests to get into the room.

"Steven told me earlier that Rylee is a psychic medium," Emily said to Joe, though she was eyeing Steven as he fiddled with a small video camera. "I expect whatever did this recognized Rylee's abilities and was trying to establish contact with her. I don't think the rest of you have anything to worry about."

In fact, Emily realized, she herself didn't feel at all worried. She was half convinced Rylee—and maybe Steven, too—had set this whole thing up. Still, she didn't want to let her suspicions show, and she told Steven to come get her in the parlor when he was done filming, so she could help put Rylee's room back together.

Emily's four other guests were grumbling as they went back to their own rooms, and she overheard Dominique say, "That's the second time a ghost has kept us from going to sleep tonight. I sure hope there's not a third time."

"Me, too," Emily said under her breath as she went downstairs.

It was nearly an hour before Steven finally came into

the parlor, where Emily was sitting on the sofa with a book. She hadn't turned the page in at least ten minutes, too absorbed in thinking about everything that had happened in the past couple of hours to focus on reading.

"We're all done," he said, smiling. "Emily, you have got to let us film here for the show! This is extraordinary!"

Emily tried to return Steven's smile as she answered, "I'll have a full house of guests this week. Unfortunately, I don't think filming will be possible." Even if her suspicions were wrong, and Rylee's room really had been trashed by a ghost, Emily still didn't want the hassle. And, if a ghost had targeted Rylee because it recognized her abilities, she didn't want to risk anything further happening. It was bad enough one set of guests was experiencing a frightening night. She didn't want the same to happen to the next group.

Steven's smile actually widened. "As a matter of fact, your guests and my talent are one and the same. Tessa and Rylee are staying here all week."

Emily tilted her head. "I think you're mistaken. I have a party arriving tomorrow, and they booked all four rooms."

"Yes, Tessa's assistant made the reservation. He'll be staying here along with the two of them."

Emily felt her heart sink. Even if she flat-out refused to allow Steven to feature Eternal Rest in the show, she would still be involved with them from Sunday all the way to the following Sunday. "And who's going to be in the fourth room?" she asked, hearing the false friendliness in her voice. "Are you continuing your stay here?"

This time, Steven's smile did falter. "No, Tessa didn't want the talent and the production team staying at the same place. She felt like sleeping in a haunted B and B should be reserved for her and Rylee. And Vic, of course, because she can't seem to function if he's not glued to her side. The fourth room will be used as an interview and séance room. Tessa wanted a pretty spot to channel ghosts and to tell the camera about her experiences without worrying her dirty underwear would accidentally wind up in the shot."

"Oh," Emily answered. It was all she could muster.

Emily trudged up the stairs behind Steven, though she perked up a little when she saw that Rylee had already started putting her room to rights. Steven helped Emily remake the bed, then all three of them picked up leaves and petals from the carpet. The work went much more quickly than Emily had anticipated, and before long, she was once again in her bedroom.

As soon as the door was shut behind her, Emily began calling out to Scott again. "Are you still there? Can you communicate through Kelly, like you did before? You called the dark entity 'she.' Can you tell me more about her?"

Emily went into the bathroom and brushed her teeth, figuring that would give Kelly enough time to chat with Scott, then write a note. When she came back out, Kelly had simply written, *He's scared. Hiding again.*

"Thanks, Kelly. Please let me know when he comes back." With a sigh, Emily flopped into bed. It took a long time for her to finally fall asleep, but as the minutes ticked past, she was grateful not to hear another peep from the entity or from her guests.

Breakfast on Sunday morning was much better than Emily had anticipated. She had expected her guests—the ones who weren't filming a TV show, at least—to be unhappy and scared, but when she came into the dining room to see if she needed to replenish anything, she found Joe and Alana talking excitedly with Tyler and Dominique. Apparently, after a good night's sleep and with sunshine streaming through the front windows, they had a different view of their experiences the night before.

Emily felt her heart lighten as they wished her a hearty good morning, then continued chatting with each other. Rylee and Steven hadn't come downstairs yet, but that was no surprise to Emily, since they had been up later than the rest of her guests.

A couple hours later, Emily was alone in the house. Steven had checked out, and Rylee tagged along as he headed to the hotel he and his production team would be staying at for the upcoming week. The two planned to get lunch in Oak Hill once Steven got settled in. The rest of Emily's guests had hit the road, too, telling her before they left how much they had enjoyed their weekend.

Emily took extra care as she cleaned the guest rooms, knowing at least one of them would be used for filming. Eternal Rest was going to show up on TV, even if she refused to let the house be featured as a haunted location. Once the cleaning was done, Emily walked to Hilltop Cemetery next door. It was a hot, sticky August afternoon, but she wanted to get out and enjoy having a guest-free house while she could. She walked to the very top of the hill and sat on a bench under the shade of an oak tree.

For weeks, Emily had sat on a bench facing west, where she had once glimpsed Scott's ghost just outside the protective psychic barrier that surrounded Oak Hill. Now that Scott was home, she chose a bench that looked toward Eternal Rest. The dark-blue clapboard house looked beautiful in summer, when the lawn and all the trees around it were green and lush.

Soon, though, it was time for Emily to return to the house to await her guests' arrival. At five o'clock, Emily was sitting at her rolltop desk in the parlor when she heard a car in the circular driveway. She took a moment to appreciate the silence of the house before rising to welcome her new guests.

Emily hadn't reached the front door yet when there was a sharp knock. She opened the door wide, expecting to see all three of her guests, and saw only a man who looked like he was in his late twenties. He was immaculately dressed in a plaid Oxford shirt and olive-green pants. Emily noticed that his loafers gleamed, as if they were freshly polished. The man reached up to adjust his wire-rimmed glasses as he eyed Emily with a judgmental frown. After a moment, he gave a curt nod. "Yes, good. You look nice."

Emily glanced down at her black jeans and dark-blue button-down shirt, which had *Eternal Rest Bed and Breakfast* embroidered in silver on the left breast. Her light-brown hair was up in a bun instead of her usual low ponytail, since it was so humid out. The last thing she wanted was her hair sticking to her neck.

"Um, thank you," Emily said tentatively. "Welcome to Eternal Rest. You're Vic Orman?"

"Tessa's assistant, yes," the man said. Emily could tell by the way he straightened his shoulders that it was a title he held with pride. "I wanted to make sure this place is acceptable before she comes in. Rylee and Steven gave it a thumbs up, but it never hurts to double-check."

Emily blinked. *Why wouldn't my house be acceptable?* She stood back and gestured for Vic to come in. He looked into the parlor and dining room, then began walking up the stairs. Hastily, Emily grabbed her key ring off her desk and followed him.

"I thought Tessa might like room one, which has a view of both Hilltop Cemetery and the front lawn," Emily said, passing Vic so she could lead him to the guest room above the parlor. She unlocked the door, opened it, and led the way inside.

Vic looked around briefly, then said, "Yes, this will do nicely. I'll bring Tessa in."

Just a few minutes later, Emily again stood at her front door, this time welcoming a woman she recognized from TV interviews. Tessa walked up the front porch steps, then froze, one hand gripping the railing.

"Oh!" she wailed. "I can sense them. Your ghosts, they're so unhappy!"

Tessa turned to Vic, who was pulling suitcases out of the trunk of a nice sedan. "Bring the camera, Vic. Right now!" As Vic scrambled to comply, Tessa reached up and patted her wavy auburn hair, then pulled a compact out of her purse and began making pouty faces at herself in the mirror. Emily wasn't surprised when Tessa produced a tube of red lipstick and reapplied it.

Vic ran up with a video camera in his hand. "Ready when you are!"

Tessa was still standing halfway up the porch steps, and she turned to face Vic. "Frame it so you can see the front door behind me." Tessa glanced over her shoulder and said to Emily, "Would you close the door, please?"

Emily had to decide which side of the door she wanted to be on. She chose to stay inside, shutting it with a polite smile before returning to her desk. She was fuming at Tessa's snap judgment about the Eternal Rest ghosts. "What could she have possibly sensed, anyway?" Emily asked herself. "She wasn't even in the house yet!"

It was another twenty minutes before the front door opened again. By then, Emily was still annoyed, but she was able to smile more genuinely this time. She might disagree with Tessa's assessment of her ghosts, but it was the first time a celebrity had stayed at Eternal Rest, and Emily couldn't help but feel excited about it.

Emily moved to the parlor doorway and introduced herself. "You'll be upstairs, in room one." Emily began to hand the key to Tessa, then thought better of it. If the woman couldn't even carry her own luggage, then she was probably expecting an escort to her room, too. "I'll take you up there. Vic, you'll be in room three, which also has a great view of Hilltop Cemetery. Rylee is already settled into room two."

As Emily led the way upstairs, Tessa said dramatically, "The unhappiness is so much stronger in here. Your poor ghosts, Emily. How they must be suffering in the afterlife!"

Emily bit her lip and remained silent. *No wonder Sage can't stand her.*

While Tessa and Vic settled into their rooms, Emily went to the kitchen to pour two glasses of sweet tea for her new guests. She wondered if Vic would require a taste test to ensure it was good enough for Tessa.

Emily had just reached the parlor with the tea when the doorbell rang. Knowing it would be Trish Alden with Emily's baked goods delivery, Emily put down the tray and rushed to open it. She needed to talk to someone normal.

"Hey, Emily," Trish said in her thick Southern accent when Emily opened the door. "How did your séance go last night?"

Emily groaned. "Not great."

"You couldn't get the ghosts to communicate? I figured Mrs. Thompson would be all for it!"

"There was communication, all right," Emily began. She heard footsteps on the stairs behind her, and she watched as Trish's face lit up with delight.

"Tessa Valentine!" Trish shouted. She immediately pulled her long blonde French braid over her shoulder and patted it self-consciously.

"Hello," Tessa said, gliding past Emily to shake Trish's hand. "And who might you be?"

"Trish Alden. I own Grainy Day Bakery on the square downtown. I'm such a big fan of yours. I have all of your books, and if Emily had told me you were staying here, I would have baked you something special." Trish was grinning, her fingers still clamped around Tessa's hand.

"A bakery? How wonderful." Tessa turned to Vic, expertly extracting her hand in the process. "Make a note of it. I want you to pick up some fresh baked goods in the morning."

"Actually, they're right here," Emily said, lifting the box Trish had just handed her. "Trish delivers them each evening for breakfast the next morning."

"Superb!" Tessa winked at Trish. "I'll have to come try some of your sweets one afternoon."

"On the house," Trish said quickly. "I think you'll love my peach tart."

"I look forward to it." Tessa turned and retreated into the parlor, leaving Trish staring after her, open-mouthed.

"Wow, Emily," Trish said. "Tessa Valentine!"

"Yeah. I didn't even know she was staying with me until earlier today."

"Well, I'd better head home." In a quieter voice, Trish said, "I want to know *everything* that happens during her stay!"

Emily had to laugh. She knew Trish would be doling out both biscuits and gossip when she opened the doors of Grainy Day the next morning.

Tessa called Emily into the hallway once Trish left. She insisted on sampling some of Trish's baking immediately, so Emily went to the kitchen to arrange some biscuits and croissants on a plate. She had ordered baked goods for four guests, not knowing one of the rooms would be unoccupied, so at least she had some to spare.

By the time she returned to the parlor, Rylee and Steven were coming through the front door. Once Emily had served the baked goods to Tessa, Steven waved her into the dining room. He shut the door behind them.

"Emily, have you given more thought to letting us film here?" Steven asked.

This time, Emily didn't hesitate. "I'd rather not, but thank you for the offer."

"Why not? Your house is haunted, and it would be great publicity for you." Steven looked confused, as if he genuinely couldn't understand Emily's refusal.

Emily thought about telling him she disliked how he and Rylee had posed as a father and daughter to secretly scout out Eternal Rest, and she realized they hadn't just been confirming it was haunted. They had also wanted to make sure it was up to Tessa's apparently high standards. Emily also thought about telling Steven she suspected Rylee had trashed her own room. Instead, what she said was, "Tessa said she felt anger from the ghosts here. That's not the kind of publicity I'm looking for."

"Maybe she can help them find peace," Steven suggested. "She can discover why they're angry and make things better."

"I'd rather not risk it. However, I'd be happy to let you look for ghosts in the cemetery. There's been some weird activity happening over there. I've heard a banging noise several times, but more importantly, I saw a shadow figure there one night. It's a beautiful cemetery with a rich history."

Steven eyed Emily doubtfully. "We'll consider it, then. In the meantime, keep thinking about my offer. We'll pay for the right to film here, of course."

Emily just gave Steven a tight smile in response.

It was a relief when Emily's guests and Steven left the house a short while later to eat dinner at a restaurant in town. Once the house was silent, Emily stood thoughtfully in the parlor, wondering if Tessa was right about her ghosts being unhappy. It had seemed ridiculous when Tessa had said it, but Emily could understand that her ghosts might not be pleased with the current situation. They were facing down the dark entity, and they were trying to protect Scott from it. Eternal Rest was no longer the safe haven it had once been for them.

By the time Emily's three guests returned, she had already eaten dinner and sorted through a few online reservation requests. She had also steeled herself for more surprising revelations from Tessa. If her ghosts really were unhappy, then Emily wanted to know why so she could try to help them.

Getting rid of the dark entity would be a good start.

Tessa was rather subdued as she came into the parlor with Vic and Rylee. Emily was still at her desk in the back corner, and as her guests began discussing their filming schedule for the next day, Emily quietly left the room.

Emily was arranging dishes on the sideboard in the dining room when she heard Vic calling her name. She went into the parlor, expecting her guests wanted more sweet tea or baked goods, and instead found Tessa sitting on the sofa with one hand pressed to her heart. She turned to Emily with raised eyebrows. "It's so crowded here," she said, sounding both surprised and offended at the same time.

Emily glanced around the room. "You're my only guests this week," she answered, even though she suspected Tessa was talking about a crowd in the ghostly sense. Even still, there were only a handful of ghosts at Eternal Rest, including the ghost of a child who rarely made their presence known. If Scott was off hiding somewhere, then that just left Mrs. Thompson, Kelly, Grandma Gray, and the child.

"Can't you sense them?" Tessa asked incredulously. "Rylee said you're a medium, too."

"I'm still learning," Emily said. "I have four ghosts here. Two ladies, a teenage girl, and a child."

"There are men here, too." Tessa rose and stared hard at one corner of the room. "Three of them, standing there in long coats and top hats. They're angry, but not at us. They're arguing... Oh! It's a dispute about whom the rightful owner of this house is."

Emily was grateful Tessa had her back to her so she couldn't see the way Emily wrinkled her nose at this pronouncement. If there were three men haunting Eternal Rest, Sage would have known it. Besides, the house had been built for the sexton of Hilltop Cemetery. There had never, to Emily's knowledge, been any debate about that.

"You're so perceptive, Tessa," Vic said encouragingly.

Rylee didn't say anything. Instead, she was staring at the same corner as Tessa, her eyes narrowed and a little frown on her face.

"There's a male ghost in my room, too," Tessa said, turning to Emily. "I felt him as soon as I walked in. I think he died in that room, maybe by his own hand. Do you know anything about that?"

"I... No," Emily stammered. Out of the corner of her eye, she could see Rylee shake her head, almost imperceptibly.

"I'll try to communicate with him tonight." Tessa squared her shoulders and stuck out her chin. "We need to make sure your future guests are safe. He didn't seem threatening, but of course, he might simply be trying to lure me into a false sense of security. I won't be able to let my guard down, even when I'm sleeping!"

Emily wanted to ask Tessa how that was even possible, then thought better of it.

Tessa heaved a sigh. "It's best to begin communicating

now, I suppose. Vic, will you please accompany me? I still have a few things to unpack."

Emily wished them a good night, but as Rylee moved to follow them, Emily motioned for her to stay. Once Emily heard Tessa's door close upstairs, she asked Rylee quietly, "You seemed to disagree with Tessa's description of the three men haunting the corner."

Rylee's cheeks flushed. "Tessa is a much more experienced medium than I am. That's why she's my mentor. She's been so kind to take me under her wing."

"It's just that Sage, whom you met Saturday night, has never sensed a male presence here," Emily continued. "Well, except for two I accidentally brought into the house —one through a photo, and one through a mirror—but both of them have crossed over. I think it's odd that Tessa has identified four ghosts that not even Sage or my resident ghosts have sensed."

Rylee glanced over her shoulder, then walked quickly to the parlor door and shut it before returning to her original spot. "I haven't sensed any male ghosts here. Not that Tessa's wrong!" Rylee held up her hands defensively. "I'm not disagreeing with her. It's just that I can only sense the women you told us about. Kelly is the one I feel the strongest, probably because I'm closest to her in age. She was in love when she died, you know."

"I know. With Dylan Williams."

"And then, of course, there's the ghost that trashed my room last night. Ghosts like that can be dangerous. I sense that she's very angry."

"Scott also indicated that the entity was female," Emily said. She gestured for Rylee to sit in one of the wingback chairs arranged around the coffee table. Once she was seated, Emily perched on the edge of the sofa, leaning toward Rylee. "Tell me everything you've experienced and sensed with this entity."

Rylee spread her hands. "You saw what she did to my room last night. It took me a long time to fall asleep once we got everything cleaned up. Tessa always says it's stupid to be afraid of ghosts, but I couldn't help it. I finally fell asleep, but then I woke up really early this morning, and I could sense she was in the room with me."

"Did the ghost try to hurt you?" Emily asked.

"No. Last night, I thought that was what the ghost wanted. I had thought what she did to my room was from anger, and that she might lash out at me next. This morning, though, since I was right there in the same room with her, I could feel emotions rolling off of her. I felt so much anger, but not like the kind I've felt with malevolent ghosts before. This seemed more petulant, like a ghost who was sick and tired of not getting her own way. Under that anger, though, I felt deep, deep sorrow."

Emily sat back and stared at her folded hands as she thought over Rylee's information. She could certainly understand why the ghost would be giving off that sort of anger: she had wanted to keep Scott bound to herself—and away from Eternal Rest—for some reason, but she had lost that battle, thanks in part to Emily herself. Emily looked up at Rylee. "How did you come to the conclusion that the ghost was female?"

Rylee hesitated. "I don't know how far you are in your mediumship development, but at some point, you learn to feel that sort of thing. It's like an impression. When it first starts happening, you'll think it's your imagination, but you have to go with it. Eventually, you'll learn to trust your instincts about details like that. This ghost is fairly young, too, I think, though I didn't get a clear sense of her age."

Emily nodded, even as she realized Rylee's details about the entity felt a lot more genuine than what Tessa had been claiming about all the additional ghosts apparently haunting Eternal Rest. For the first time, Emily began to believe Rylee's room really had been wrecked by the entity, rather than by Rylee herself as some kind of publicity stunt.

"I still don't understand why it—she—didn't do any real damage to your room," Emily said. "If I was an angry ghost, I probably would have started by throwing anything breakable."

"I considered that, too. I'm starting to think her anger isn't directed at me, and she was just trying to get my attention. Like you said yourself last night, maybe she knows I'm a medium, so she's hoping to communicate with me."

Emily leaned forward again and looked at Rylee earnestly. "Be careful. If you decide to open yourself up to her, you need to take precautions first. Shield yourself spiritually. Your instincts about her might be correct, but she behaved toward both me and Sage in a way that was utterly terrifying."

Rylee raised an eyebrow. "Maybe the ghost is angry with the two of you, then."

"Considering we're part of the group responsible for getting Scott home, I'm sure she's very angry with us."

Rylee rose. "Then you need to be shielding yourself, too. I'm going to bed. We'll be filming all day tomorrow, and I need to make sure I'm well rested and ready to communicate with whatever ghosts we come across."

"Good night, Rylee, and thank you. Please let me know if you learn anything else about the ghost."

Emily had a hard time concentrating on her tasks when she went into the kitchen. She stood in front of the coffee maker for a solid three minutes, just staring into the empty filter she had put into it. It was a light tap against the doorframe that brought her attention back to the present moment.

Vic was standing there, and Emily nearly laughed, seeing his starched and pressed striped pajamas. He was wearing matching blue slippers. *He even dresses nice when he's sleeping*, she thought.

"Oh, I'm glad I caught you when I did," Vic said. "Tessa has a few requirements for her breakfast."

Emily frowned. "Did she not like the biscuits and croissants she had earlier?"

"Oh, she loved those. But she's had a bit of, ah, stomach trouble lately. She's trying a vegetarian diet, and she's drinking herbal tea in the morning instead of coffee. You do have herbal tea, I hope?"

"I have several options. I'll put the kettle on in the morning, and Tessa can choose whichever one she prefers."

"And I saw on your website that you serve a Continental breakfast, so please leave any meat products out of it during our stay."

Emily had welcomed plenty of guests with dietary

requests, but Vic's caught her off guard. "Oh, are you and Rylee also vegetarian?"

"No." Vic hesitated, then glanced quickly down the hallway before saying in an undertone, "It's just, well, I try as hard as I can to keep Tessa happy. Sometimes that means the rest of us have to make a sacrifice or two."

After what she had already seen of Tessa, there was nothing surprising in Vic's admission, and Emily put on her best sympathetic face. "You're a very dedicated assistant," she said.

"I try," Vic said, though any attempt at humility was ruined by his smug smile.

Emily put several varieties of herbal tea on the countertop before heading to bed, just to make sure she wouldn't forget in the morning. Once she was in her bedroom, Emily was already in her pajamas—after seeing Vic's, she felt downright shabby wearing an old T-shirt of Scott's and a pair of cotton shorts—before she saw Kelly had left her a note on the dresser.

We're not unhappy, Emily. We love it here. Just worried about Scott.

"So you overheard all of that earlier?" Emily asked. She shook her head at herself in the mirror. In a quieter voice, she said, "She's a bit ridiculous, isn't she?"

The next morning, Emily had arranged breakfast on the sideboard, including the teapot and a selection of teas, before her guests had come downstairs. Once she heard them file into the dining room, she remained at her desk for another five minutes, giving them a chance to settle in, then went into the dining room to wish them a good morning.

Emily's greeting died on her lips as soon as she entered the dining room. Tessa was sprawled back in her chair, one hand covering her eyes, as she moaned softly. Vic was hurrying to close the curtains, and Emily realized he had already turned off the lights. Rylee was biting into a biscuit smothered with strawberry jam, apparently unconcerned with the situation.

"Are you okay, Tessa?" Emily asked.

"You can send me to the guillotine," she answered in a weary voice. "It would be a blessing to have this thing lopped off my neck."

Emily glanced at Vic, who moved closer to her and whispered, "She has a terrible headache this morning."

"Can I get her anything? A cold compress or something?" Emily spoke in a whisper, too. She knew how valuable peace and quiet were when one had a headache, though she wasn't sure why Tessa had bothered to come downstairs at all if she felt so terrible.

"She took something for it already. She's hoping a little breakfast and tea will help." Vic actually looked slightly apologetic, and Emily wondered just how far his tolerance for Tessa's dramatics went.

"You and Rylee are welcome to eat at the kitchen table so Tessa can have some privacy," Emily whispered.

Emily wondered if Tessa had supernatural hearing or if she was using her psychic abilities as she wailed, "Don't leave me alone in here."

Emily figured it was futile to suggest Tessa go back upstairs to lie down. She seemed to want the attention, no matter how bad she felt. Instead, Emily simply tiptoed out of the room and walked straight out the front door. She figured she could water the plants in the side yard, where she could make noise without disturbing Tessa.

A flash of light from the direction of the two-lane road that Eternal Rest sat on attracted Emily's attention as she walked down the porch steps. Someone was standing on her front lawn, holding up a sign. The white poster board had caught the sun and reflected it toward Emily. She had the silly, fleeting thought that Detective Danny Hernandez had come to declare his affection for her with some big gesture, but she quickly realized it wasn't him. She also realized it was a ridiculous idea.

Curious but cautious, Emily slowly began walking toward the person. As she got closer, she could see it was a woman with a long brown braid hanging over one shoulder. Her jeans had several smears of paint that matched the wording on the sign. It read, *Go home, heretic!*

How did Vic not see this woman when he closed the dining room curtains? Emily wondered. *Or maybe he did, but he didn't want to upset Tessa.*

It was clear to Emily that this sign had to be about Tessa, since she was the only person at Eternal Rest who was well known. Emily stopped about twenty feet away from the woman and said loudly, "May I help you?"

"You can help me by getting that sinner out of your house!" The woman's face was pinched in anger.

"We're all sinners, I suppose," Emily said, folding her arms. "Which one do you mean?"

"I mean that horrible Tessa Valentine, of course! She showed up in Oak Hill yesterday to spread her lies and evil. It's bad enough this town already has one person who claims to consort with the dead."

Emily actually laughed, since the woman had no idea she was talking to a budding medium that very moment. The woman's face grew more red, and finally she shouted, "You're letting her stay under your roof! You're just as bad if you're knowingly sheltering a so-called *psychic!*" She spat out the last word as if it were vulgar.

Emily's mirth dissolved as she realized this was the kind of hatred Sage had to endure. "My best friend is a psychic medium," she said pointedly. "Tessa is here for work, and I will not allow her to be harassed by you or anyone."

"I'm allowed to protest!"

"Yes, you are, but not on my private property." Emily

made a little shooing motion with her hands. Grumbling, the woman walked backward until her feet were on the edge of the road.

Emily had thought she would give up and go home, not simply step off Eternal Rest property, and she hoped the woman wouldn't wind up getting run over in her eagerness to protest Tessa's presence. With a frustrated huff, Emily turned and walked back to the house. She looked back at the woman just before going inside; she was still standing on the road, her sign raised high.

"We have a little situation," Emily began as she went into the dining room. She was trying to keep her voice quiet so she wouldn't exacerbate Tessa's headache, but it was hard when she felt so riled up.

"You mean the protester?" Tessa asked. Her voice sounded stronger, and she was sitting up a little straighter in her chair. "We spotted her when Vic cracked the curtains a bit so we could see our breakfast better."

"I'm so sorry about this," Emily said. "I can call the police, though she's not on my lawn anymore, and I don't know if they can do anything."

"Oh, no," Tessa said quickly. "Let her stand out there in the sweltering heat as long as she likes. I might even have Vic take a picture of her for my social media."

Of course she's not upset about it, Emily told herself. *It's just another way of getting attention.*

Emily tensed when the doorbell rang, wondering if the protester had followed her up to the house to confront Tessa face-to-face. When she looked out the peephole, though, Emily spied a man standing there. She opened the door and saw he was holding a giant bouquet of roses.

Someone sent me flowers!

"Hi, there," he said, his white teeth flashing in his tanned face. He pulled off his dark sunglasses to reveal sparkling blue eyes. "I'm here for Tessa Valentine."

6

Before Emily could respond, she heard a shriek behind her. She turned to see Tessa standing in the hallway, the palms of her hands pressed together and a delighted smile on her face. "Brian!"

The man brushed past Emily as he walked into the house. "Tessa, darling. Surprise! And happy six-month anniversary!"

"Oh, you shouldn't have!" Tessa reached out and plucked the bouquet from Brian's hand. She lowered her face toward the blooms and gave an exaggerated sniff. "Roses. My favorite! Vic, put these in a vase, then place them on the dresser in my room. Make sure they catch the sunlight nicely."

It was only after Tessa had handed the flowers off to Vic that she finally leaned forward and pressed her lips to Brian's cheek. "You drove all the way from Louisville to surprise me with flowers?" she gushed.

Brian lifted his chin proudly. "I did. But, since I'm here now, I thought I might stay with you this week."

"Of course you're staying!" Tessa said, smacking Brian's arm playfully. "You think I would make you turn around and go home after a surprise like this? What kind of a terrible girlfriend do you think I am?"

"The worst," Brian said with a wink.

Emily was staring at the entire exchange, open-mouthed, when Vic nudged her with his elbow. "Do you have a vase I can borrow?" he asked.

"Of course," Emily said. "Come on, I've got a few in the kitchen cabinet."

Tessa's exuberant voice carried all the way into the kitchen, and as Emily began rummaging around in a bottom cabinet for a vase big enough for the bouquet, she realized Tessa's headache certainly didn't seem to be troubling her anymore.

The kitchen suddenly became much quieter, and Emily looked up to see that Vic had closed the door behind him. Even though he couldn't see down the hallway, he was staring in the direction of the front door. His nostrils flared, and his fingers squeezed the bouquet. "Ow!" Vic shook one hand. "Stupid thorns."

"I take it you weren't expecting Brian, either?" Emily asked.

Vic finally turned to Emily. "No. In fact, I totally understand if you need to charge us extra since he'll be staying with us."

Emily shrugged as she stood up, a green cut-glass vase in her hands. "I already charged you for a fourth person, since you booked the fourth room. I even ordered enough baked goods each morning for four people. It's really not a problem."

Vic's eyes narrowed. "It might be. I'll be spending the rest of my week trying to keep the two of them apart as much as possible."

"Oh?" Emily asked casually as she placed the vase under the faucet and began to fill it with water.

Vic was silent for a long while. Finally, he said, "She's here to work."

Emily reached out and took the roses from Vic. She wasn't sure if he simply disliked Brian, or if he really was a distraction for Tessa. As she trimmed the stems of the roses and began arranging them in the vase, another thought struck her: maybe Vic was jealous. When Brian wasn't around, Emily could clearly see that Vic was Tessa's number one man. She didn't treat him well, but she did make him feel needed.

"Where are you filming today?" Emily asked, wanting to steer the conversation to something Vic might not be so angry about.

"A place called Tanner's Mill. From the photos, I expect it will be full of ticks and broken glass."

"The old mill is actually a nice spot to visit. The buildings are right on the edge of a pretty little creek. I thought everything was boarded up, though. Is Tessa planning to communicate with the ghosts through the brick walls?"

"The owner of the property is letting us go inside a few of the buildings that are still structurally sound. At first, he suggested everyone wear hard hats, just in case. Can you imagine Tessa wearing a hard hat—on camera, no less?" Vic laughed heartily.

"No, I can't imagine," Emily said, not able to hide her own smile as she handed Vic the vase.

"Thank you, Emily." Vic raised the vase like he was giving a toast before leaving the kitchen and, presumably, heading upstairs to arrange the vase just so on Tessa's dresser.

Emily had planned to return to the parlor, but instead, she found herself standing in the hallway and face-to-face with Steven Bates, who had just come in the front door. Steeling herself for a renewal of his request to film at Eternal Rest, Emily plastered on a smile and wished him a good morning.

"I'm not sure it is," Steven answered. "Emily, Tessa has a lot of fans, but that's not who's out there on your lawn."

"Oh, I know. I went out and talked to her this morning,

but as long as she's not actually standing on my property, I don't think I can do anything. Besides, Tessa seemed kind of excited to be the target of a disgruntled protestor."

"You might want to take a look outside," Steven said. He turned and opened the front door, then pointed toward the lawn.

The single protester had turned into about a dozen. They were standing in a cluster, right in the middle of Emily's front yard.

Emily swore under her breath. "Shut the door," she told Steven. "I'll take care of this." She was already pulling out her cell phone while she spoke.

There was only one ring before Emily heard a smooth voice say, "Good morning, Emily. I haven't talked to you in a while."

"Hi, Danny."

Detective Danny Hernandez must have heard something in Emily's voice, because his tone instantly changed to one of concern. "What's wrong? Are you in danger?"

"No, but I have a gaggle of protesters in my front yard. I told their ringleader they couldn't be on my property, but, apparently, someone with a uniform needs to tell them."

Emily could hear the confusion in Danny's voice as he answered, "Protesters? Is this about one of the murder cases you've been involved in?"

"I'm afraid it's even more scandalous than murder." Emily smiled at the phone. Danny was jumping to the worst-case scenario, and it reminded Emily that a few upset people with signs wasn't nearly as bad as being involved in a murder investigation. "I've got a celebrity psychic staying here this week. Apparently, word got out, and the moral police are not happy about it."

"I'll send somebody around. In fact—hang on." There was a *clunk*, followed by Danny's voice calling, as if from a distance, "Hey, Roger! Emily needs a hand with some trespassers. You up for it?" There was another thud, then Danny sounded normal again. "Roger is on his way. In the meantime, what are you doing for lunch? I can pick you up and take you into town."

"Thanks, but I've got work to do here. Apparently, one of my rooms will be used for filming segments of a new TV show. I want to make sure everything looks nice." Emily breathed a silent sigh of relief that she had come up with an excuse so quickly. She liked Danny, and he was proving to be a good friend, but she didn't want to get involved with anyone romantically at the moment. Even if he hadn't been asking her out on a formal date, she still expected his invitation wasn't strictly a friendly one.

It had been a week since Emily and Danny had talked, and if he felt like she was avoiding him, then he was right. Even after promising to back off on any talk of romance, Danny still seemed determined to wear Emily down.

"I need to let my guests know that Officer Newton is on his way. Thank you, Danny," Emily said.

"You're welcome, Emily," Danny answered, unable to keep the note of disappointment out of his voice.

Emily had only just finished making the rounds of her guests' rooms, letting them know to expect company, when the doorbell rang. Roger Newton had an amused smile on his face when Emily answered the door. "Well, Miss Emily, I'm glad to see you've moved from dead bodies to simple trespassing."

"Hi, Officer New—Roger, I mean. It appears a few folks in Oak Hill disapprove of one of my guests."

Roger chuckled. "I heard all about it on the way in. I was told that I'm walking into a bona fide den of iniquity."

"How scandalous of you," Emily teased.

"I'll have them off your property in the time it takes you to fix me a sweet tea." Roger patted his close-cropped blond hair, which was graying at the temples. "It's hot out."

"Deal."

Roger was true to his word: no sooner had Emily brought two sweet teas into the parlor than Roger knocked on the door again. Emily glanced past him to see that the group of protesters was breaking up. "Come on in," she said. "I want to know how you did that so easily."

It wasn't until Roger had sat down on the sofa and taken a long drink of tea before he put his glass down and said, "One of the folks out there is my cousin Denny. I reminded him that he's no saint, either, and that I could tell a few tales that would get everyone to start making signs about *him*. After that, it was easy to talk them into leaving. Living in a small town does have its perks."

"I appreciate your help. We all do."

Roger turned his eyes toward the hallway as footsteps sounded down the stairs. "I didn't do it for some famous lady, and frankly, I'm not sure I care to meet her. We don't exactly have a lot in common. Thanks for the tea, Miss Emily."

Emily followed Roger into the hallway, where he stopped abruptly. His gaze was fixed on the stairs, his eyebrows scrunched down in concentration. Emily's eyes flicked from Roger's alert face to the staircase. "Roger, what is it?"

"You heard them, right? The footsteps? They were coming down the stairs, and they got to the bottom right as I got to the doorway."

Emily nearly clapped her hands in delight. Roger, the staunch skeptic, had experienced something paranormal. "But there's no one there," she prompted.

Roger sniffed. "Probably just weird echoes or something." He turned and headed toward the front door, and as he let himself out, Emily heard him mutter, "Sound effects... Hidden speakers... Gotta be something like that."

Oh, well. I guess it's going to take more than phantom footsteps for Roger to turn into a believer.

Emily tapped one foot anxiously while she sat at her desk, waiting for her guests to leave for the day. When they had all finally left in a flurry of makeup cases, garment bags full of spare outfits, and shouted demands from Tessa, Emily ran to the sofa, closed her eyes, and called, "Scott? Was that you on the stairs?"

After half an hour, Emily finally gave up trying to establish contact with Scott. Whatever had made that sound on the stairs, it wasn't his ghost. Feeling frustrated, Emily returned to her desk. At some point, Kelly had written a note on the paper by Emily's laptop: *He's still hiding. I can't tell you where, because the scary ghost might see.*

"Thanks, Kelly."

The rest of Emily's day passed swiftly. She cleaned the guest rooms, taking extra care with the empty one that Tessa wanted to use for filming, and she even spruced up the parlor and dining room a bit. After meeting Tessa and learning how demanding she was, it seemed like the best course of action.

When Trish stopped by in the late afternoon, she nearly threw the Grainy Day baked goods at Emily in her rush. She had her phone up to one ear, sandwiched between her head and her shoulder, and her eyes had a faraway look. Whatever she was seeing, it wasn't Emily.

"Okay, that's a lot of cupcakes in a short amount of time, but I can do it," Trish said into the phone. Finally, her eyes snapped to Emily, and she mouthed, "Hey. Sorry!"

Emily just gave Trish a reassuring wave, though she expected Trish's brief stop that evening meant a much longer one the next day: Emily knew her friend would want every little tidbit of information about Tessa she could get.

It was a little after eight o'clock before Emily's guests returned to Eternal Rest. Rylee was the first, and after a brief hello to Emily, she went upstairs to her room. Brian came in about twenty minutes later, going upstairs silently.

Vic bustled in shortly after Brian, a shopping bag in one hand and a frazzled expression on his face. He appeared in the doorway of the parlor. "Hi, Emily. What a long day! I'm going to bed." Without waiting for a response, he disappeared, his weary footsteps echoing up the stairs.

Five minutes later, Brian and Vic came downstairs together, and as they filed into the parlor, Emily noticed with a start that Brian's worried expression matched Vic's.

"Where is Tessa?" Vic asked tersely.

"Did she come back with Rylee?" Brian asked Emily.

Emily shook her head as she stood up from her desk, feeling a sudden stab of worry. "No, Tessa hasn't come back yet. Weren't you all together today?"

Vic raised the shopping bag that was still clutched in one hand. "I had to drive halfway to Atlanta today to find her favorite makeup brand," he said. "Brian and I just tried calling her, but her phone didn't even ring. It went straight to voicemail for both of us."

"Maybe Rylee knows where Tessa is," Emily suggested.

Brian turned on his heel and nearly sprinted up the stairs. A few seconds later, Emily heard him banging loudly and calling, "Rylee!"

Soon, Brian came back into the parlor, followed by a confused-looking Rylee. "What's going on?" she asked, stifling a yawn.

"Tessa hasn't come back yet," Emily said. "Okay, Vic, you said you left to go shopping. Was Tessa still with the film crew at the mill at that time?"

Vic nodded. "Yeah, she was the one who asked me to go."

"Brian and Rylee, which one of you was the last to leave the mill?" Emily asked.

Rylee glanced doubtfully at Brian. "I think I was. But

she was riding in your car, Brian, so didn't she leave with you?"

Brian's forehead creased, and his eyebrows drew together. "She rode with me this morning, but I thought she left in your car, Rylee. You and Tessa were going to have a planning dinner tonight to discuss tomorrow's filming."

"We were supposed to have dinner, but she said she was going to go out with you, instead," Rylee answered. She was eyeing Brian suspiciously.

Brian turned his head and scratched the back of his neck. "She asked me to go find a good vegetarian restaurant for dinner, but I had thought that was for tomorrow night. I grabbed dinner on my own."

Emily frowned, though a part of her wanted to laugh that Brian had actually expected to find a vegetarian restaurant in the small town of Oak Hill.

"Well, whomever she left with," Rylee said, "she was gone by the time the crew got done filming me giving a summary of our day. It was just me, Steven, and a couple of crew members still out there."

Vic pulled his cell phone out of his pocket. "I'm calling Steven." He paced in front of the parlor windows while he had a brief conversation with Steven, and he looked worried as he ended the call and turned to Brian and Rylee. "Steven says he was the last to leave the site today, and Tessa was definitely not there."

"She doesn't have her own car here with her, and she certainly didn't just wander off into the woods by the mill," Rylee said. She looked at Emily. "What should we do?"

Emily said a silent prayer that Tessa would turn up soon and said, "We should call the police."

Danny arrived less than twenty minutes after Emily had called him. Emily was used to seeing him dressed for work, not in the fitted black T-shirt and jeans that he arrived in. He fixed his brown eyes on Emily worriedly when she answered the door. "I know what you're thinking, Emily," he said quietly. "Remember, this is a missing person, not a murder victim."

Emily waved Danny inside. "Then let's hope we find her soon."

Danny sat down in the parlor with Rylee, Vic, and Brian, and they all reiterated what they had already told Emily: none of them had seen Tessa leave the old mill, and no one could reach her by phone. Eventually, Danny said, "I'm going to have a couple of officers drive out to the mill to look around. In the meantime, I'll head to the hotel where the production team is staying and have a chat with them. I want three of you to split up and check local restaurants, Sutter's Bar, anywhere she might be. Emily can make a list of places to look for Tessa. One of you needs to stay here, in case she comes back."

Rylee quickly volunteered to stay at Eternal Rest, and even before Danny was gone, Emily was already seated at her desk, making a list of all the places in Oak Hill that might still be open at that time of night. Most of the restaurants would be closing up soon, but Sutter's would definitely still be open, and there were a few late-night places out near the Interstate.

Once her list was complete, Emily used it to write out three smaller lists. When she was done, she handed one each to Vic and Brian. "Vic, you'll be checking these places on the west side of town. Brian, you're taking the Interstate area. I think it's unlikely Tessa would be way out there, but it's worth checking." Emily waved the third list. "I'm taking the east side of town. Danny already gave you his card, so call him first if you learn anything, then call me: I've written my cell phone number on your lists. The maps on your phones should get you where you need to go, but call me if you get lost."

Brian and Vic left through the front door, and Emily went out the back since her car was parked under the carport behind the house. As she drove to her first stop, This is a Stickup, she tapped the steering wheel anxiously. Danny had been right: Emily was worried this wasn't simply a case of a missing person. "Please let us find her," Emily repeated over and over again as she drove.

The front door of the restaurant was locked when Emily arrived, but she saw a few people cleaning tables inside. She knocked on the glass door until a sleepy-looking teenage girl came and unlocked it for her.

"I'm looking for a woman named Tessa Valentine," Emily began. She was already searching online for a photo of her when the girl said, "The medium?"

"Yes, exactly. She was filming in town today, and we're not sure where she went afterward."

"She didn't eat here," the girl said in a disappointed tone. "I would have recognized her right away. My mom and I love her."

Emily nodded grimly. "Okay, but let me know if you hear anything, please. You can call me at Eternal Rest Bed and Breakfast."

The girl's eyes widened, as if the gravity of the situation had finally sunk in. "I will. I hope you find her."

Seeing an opportunity, Emily added, "And call your friends, if you're willing. Maybe one of them has seen her."

"On it," the girl promised.

Emily's next stop was The Stomping Grounds, which was close enough to This is a Stickup that she could just walk. As she skirted one side of the square in the middle of downtown Oak Hill, her eyes roved back and forth. *Maybe,* she tried to tell herself, *Tessa is just out for a walk, looking for more ghosts.*

The Stomping Grounds was in an old house just off

the square. During the day, it was a coffee shop, but at night, it was a wine bar. Emily saw a few people sitting at the tables on the front porch, and she felt a flicker of hope.

Emily looked closely at each person on the porch, but Tessa wasn't among them. Inside, it was hard to spot anyone from a distance because of the low lighting and dark, cozy corners. Emily headed straight for the bar and asked the man there if he had seen Tessa. He didn't recognize the name, but the woman sitting to Emily's right did.

"The psychic medium? I'd heard she was in town." The woman gave her dark hair a little fluff, as if she wanted to look nice in case Tessa came walking through the door. "She hasn't been here. I worked the afternoon shift, and then I stayed to hang out, and I can promise you, Tessa Valentine has not been through that door. If she had been, I would have posted it on my social media already."

Emily gasped. *Social media! Of course!* She thanked the woman and hurried out to the sidewalk, where it was quieter, so she could call Danny. When he answered, she said excitedly, "Has anyone checked Tessa's social media? She posts quite a lot, and maybe there's something there that will help us know where she is."

"I've said before that you would be a good detective," Danny said. "That's a smart idea, but I've already checked. Her last post was from this morning: a photo of the protesters being escorted off your lawn by Roger. He's going to love that."

"Darn. Okay, I've checked two places already, but no luck. I'll keep trying," Emily promised.

The remaining places on Emily's list were dead ends, too. They were all restaurants, and they were all already closed for the night. She drove home as the feeling of worry mounted.

Emily was the first to arrive back at Eternal Rest, less than an hour after she had left to begin the search. She felt awful having to tell Rylee that she hadn't been able to locate Tessa. Vic arrived just a few minutes after Emily. When he came into the parlor, he just shook his head sadly.

Brian finally came back half an hour later, and Danny was right on his heels as he came in the door. "I appreciate all of you helping in the search," Danny told them. "Unfortunately, Steven and the rest of the crew said they didn't notice when Tessa left the mill today. We're going to escalate things on our end. In the meantime, try to get as much rest as you can, and call me the second she shows up." He didn't need to add *if she shows up*. That part was clear from his tone and his expression.

Emily figured sleep would be elusive. She looked at her watch and was startled to see it wasn't even eleven o'clock yet. While Danny answered a few questions—mostly from Brian, who seemed to want to know every detail of what was being done to find his girlfriend—Emily pulled out her phone and texted Sage, *Keep an eye out for a missing medium. Tessa disappeared from the filming location today.*

Emily was walking Danny to the door when her phone rang, and she looked at the caller ID to see it was Sage. "Hey," Emily answered, "Danny is going to keep the search for Tessa going."

"He doesn't need to," Sage answered. "Tessa didn't disappear, Em. I picked her up at the mill this afternoon and drove her into town."

Emily was so stunned she nearly shouted into the phone. "You did what? I thought you didn't even like her! Wait, don't tell me. Not yet. Hang on." Emily called Danny's name as she put her phone on speaker. "Okay, Sage, Danny can hear you now, too. Tell me again what you just said."

"I said Tessa didn't disappear," Sage said, sounding slightly surprised. "I drove her from the mill into town earlier, around three thirty or so."

"Where is she now?" Emily asked. At the same time, Danny said, "Where did you take her?"

"I dropped her off at Under the Covers," Sage answered, "but they would have closed hours ago. Do you mean to tell me no one has seen her since then?"

"That's exactly what it seems like," Danny answered grimly. "I wonder why Tessa wanted to go to the bookstore."

"I have no idea. She didn't tell me," Sage said.

"At any rate, we can ask the shop's employees about her visit," Emily said hopefully. "Maybe they'll have an idea where she went afterward."

"I'll see if I can track down anyone from the shop tonight. I'm sure I know somebody who knows somebody that works there. Thanks for this info, Sage." Danny gave

Emily's arm a squeeze and looked at her with a mix of worry and reassurance. "Call me if she shows up," he said again.

"Of course." Once Danny was out the front door, Emily continued her conversation with Sage. She took the call off speakerphone before asking in an incredulous voice, "Why did Tessa call you, of all people, to pick her up?"

"I wish I knew, Em. She called me at Seeing Beyond, so she must have looked up the number. She said she wanted to smooth things over, and she asked if I would come pick her up. I didn't really believe she wanted to make things right with me, but I agreed, anyway. I guess I was too curious to say no."

"What did you two talk about on the drive?"

"Nothing important. She asked me to take her to the bookstore, then she talked about how active the ghosts at the mill had been, and how exhausted she was. There was something off about her. That diva persona had completely fallen away. At the time, I thought she was just awkward about being in close confines with me, given our history, but now…"

"Now, you think there might have been more going on," Emily finished.

"Yeah. She seemed distracted, almost vulnerable. I probably should have called you so you could keep an eye on her, but a client came in right after I got back to Seeing Beyond, and it just slipped my mind."

Emily frowned into the phone. "I thought you weren't seeing clients right now."

"I'm not. Rather, I'm not doing business with clients right now, since my psychic abilities are kaput. Some of them still come in, just to chat. I think they like the company and to know they're with someone who doesn't judge them for believing in the paranormal."

"That's sweet."

"I guess it is. I really wish my abilities were working, though, because I would love to know what's going on with Tessa. I don't like her, but that doesn't mean I want anything bad to happen to her."

"What happened between you two, anyway?"

"As I told you before, I'm saving that story for when we're sitting down with drinks in our hands. Good night, Em. Keep me posted."

Emily had still been standing in the hallway, and when she hung up, she realized everyone in the parlor was staring at her, listening to her conversation. She shook her head slightly as she told them Sage had dropped Tessa off at a local bookshop hours ago, and she had no idea where she might have gone after that.

"What's being done now?" Brian asked. His shirt was half untucked, and he had been tugging at his hair so much that it stuck out at crazy angles, making him look slightly wild.

"Detective Hernandez is going to try to track down someone from the shop. I'm sorry there's not more we can do."

Everyone grumbled, but there were no arguments. Vic stood slowly. "I'm going to get as much rest as I can, so I can start searching for Tessa again in the morning." He looked at Emily sadly. "I suppose Steven shouldn't have worried so much about where we were going to film this week."

Emily didn't know what words of comfort to say. She had dealt with death plenty of times, but someone who had simply vanished was a new experience for her.

Except, Emily thought, *it's not. Dylan Williams disappeared when we were in high school.*

Emily inhaled sharply, then faked a yawn to cover it. She didn't want to get everyone's hopes up in case her idea didn't lead to anything. Soon, her guests went upstairs. Brian brought up the rear, moving slowly and stopping to look over his shoulder toward the front door with every step.

The second Emily had the downstairs to herself, she went into her bedroom and called Trevor Williams. It was on the fourth ring, and Emily was preparing to leave a voicemail, when Trevor's sleepy voice answered, "Emily, what's wrong?"

"How did you know?"

"You never call me this late. In fact, you're usually in bed long before now. Something happened."

"One of my guests is missing."

All traces of sleepiness disappeared from Trevor's voice. "What can I do to help?"

"Well, we tried checking local bars and restaurants, but we didn't have any luck. I know Dylan and Kelly used to have some secluded spots around town where they would meet up secretly. Do you know where those might have been?"

"Dylan was pretty tight-lipped about all of that. Kids used to go hang out on the pier on Lake Otto in the middle of the night, though. Then there was that empty lot in the forest north of town, where that old cabin had burned down."

"Those would be shots in the dark," Emily said, disappointed.

"Why don't you ask Kelly?"

Emily pressed a palm to her forehead. "Of course! Thanks, Trevor. I'll talk to you later!"

"Wait, wait, wait!" Trevor's words ran together, and Emily heard them in time to bring the phone back up to her ear. "Are you planning to go out looking for your missing guest right now?"

"Of course."

"Emily, you are not going out to those remote places, by yourself, in the middle of the night."

"But—"

"No buts! You talk to Kelly, and by the time you have a list of places to look, I'll be at your house. I don't want to ring the doorbell and wake up your guests, so just walk outside, and I'll be waiting."

Emily smiled despite her fear. "Thanks, Trevor. See you soon."

As soon as she put down her phone, Emily called, "Kelly, did you hear that conversation? I want to know some places around town where you and Dylan met up in secret. You know, good hiding places, where Tessa could possibly be right now."

But if she's hiding, then why? What—or whom—is she afraid of?

Those thoughts occupied Emily's mind while she sat cross-legged on her bed with her eyes closed. She knew when Kelly was done writing because the pen fell to the dresser with a thud, as if Kelly had put it down with force to signal Emily.

There were three places listed on the sheet of paper. One of them looked like a very good bet: Mountain View Manor. Steven had mentioned they had wanted to film there, before finding out it was no longer haunted. That meant there was a good chance Tessa had heard about the old resort. She would have known it was secluded and abandoned: an ideal place to hide.

Emily wrote a note for her guests that she was going out and taped it to the parlor doorway, just in case someone came downstairs looking for her. She grabbed a flashlight and bug spray, then slipped out the front door as quietly as she could.

Trevor was there, just as he'd promised. He had pulled up right in front of the house, and he was leaning against the passenger door, his arms and legs crossed. For a brief moment, Emily felt like a teenager sneaking out of the house to meet up with a boy, even though she had never done anything like that in high school.

Emily gave Trevor a quick hug. "Thanks," she said again.

Once they were in Trevor's car, Emily gave him directions to Mountain View Manor, then asked, "Did I wake you up when I called earlier?"

"I was just starting to drift off." Trevor reached up and patted his thick, dark hair. "See? I don't even have bed head yet."

Emily fell silent after that, and even though Trevor glanced at her worriedly several times, he seemed to know Emily wasn't in the mood for conversation. She had her hands in her lap, her fingers twisting nervously together.

It was a strange feeling when Trevor drove around a curve in the road that led to Mountain View Manor, and Emily had her first glimpse of the pink-stuccoed Spanish Revival resort in months. She hadn't been back since crossing over three ghosts there.

Mountain View Manor was spooky enough in the daylight, but in the glow of the waxing moon, it seemed downright ominous. Emily had to remind herself that it was no longer haunted, and there was nothing to worry about.

Emily hopped out of the car as soon as Trevor pulled to a stop in the parking lot, and she made a beeline for the path that led through an overgrown garden to the front entrance. When she got there, she saw the doors had been covered with huge pieces of plywood. If Tessa was inside, then she hadn't gotten in that way.

"Come on," Emily said. Trevor had just caught up to her as she turned left to skirt the building. "There's a side door over here."

Emily was able to quickly pick a clear path through the weeds since she had a flashlight, but she heard Trevor stumble and swear behind her. She slowed her pace and let him come closer so he could see the way, too.

When they reached the side door, Emily gave it a tug, but it was locked up tight. Renovation on the hotel had ceased, after a brief attempt to restore the resort to its former glory, when one of the investors had died at the hands of his partner. It was no wonder rumors swirled that Mountain View Manor was cursed. Still, someone had made an effort to secure the building after the project had shut down.

Even while Emily was pulling on the door in vain, Trevor had continued walking, heading toward the back of the building. He was able to move faster since the path was less overgrown, and he had already turned the corner when Emily finally caught up to him.

She lunged forward and grabbed Trevor's arm. "Stop!"

Trevor turned back and looked at Emily questioningly.

"There's an empty swimming pool back here. I don't want you to fall in and break your neck." Even as she said that, Emily worried it might have happened to Tessa. She walked to the edge of the old pool and shined her flashlight around, but it was full of nothing but weeds and a puddle of water from the last storm.

The back doors had also been boarded up.

"I don't think Tessa is here," Emily said, disappointed. "I knew looking for her in places like this was a stretch, but still..."

"I know," Trevor said sympathetically. "You never want to give up on finding someone."

Trevor and Emily completed their lap of Mountain View Manor, but there was nowhere someone could have snuck in. The resort was shut up tight.

The other two places on Kelly's list were much less

likely spots for Tessa to be hiding, and Emily didn't have much hope as Trevor drove to them. One was out behind the football field at Oak Hill High School, and the other, as it turned out, didn't exist anymore. Kelly had directed Emily to an abandoned warehouse on the road that led between Oak Hill and the Interstate, but when she and Trevor arrived, it was a clear-cut lot with a sign that read, *New shopping center coming soon!*

Emily felt sick to her stomach when Trevor dropped her off at Eternal Rest. He said something comforting to her, but Emily was too lost in thought to hear his words. She felt like she was giving up on Tessa as she crawled into bed, and she hoped Danny was having better luck.

9

Emily was up before the sun on Tuesday morning. The first thing she did was check her phone, but she had no texts and no missed calls, which probably meant Danny hadn't had any success.

While Emily had been anxious to get out of bed, her guests seemed to be coping with Tessa's disappearance in the opposite way. Vic and Rylee didn't come downstairs for breakfast until shortly after eight, and Brian joined them half an hour later. Emily reluctantly told them she had no news to share.

"What are we supposed to do now?" Rylee asked. She was looking at Vic.

"We wait," he answered, reaching out to squeeze Rylee's hand.

Emily had returned to her desk in the parlor when she heard the front door open. At first, her heart soared, thinking Tessa had come back. A quick glance at the clock, though, dashed her hopes. It was nine, which meant it was Clint Alden arriving for his Tuesday shift as Emily's assistant.

Clint was no sooner in the front door than Emily appeared in the hallway, waving at him to follow her into the kitchen. Once they were inside, she shut the door, poured cups of coffee for the both of them, and sat down at the kitchen table to fill him in on the current situation.

"My mom has been talking about her nonstop," Clint said, shaking his head. "She was so excited to finally meet her. Mom might hear some valuable gossip that will help the police, so I'll talk to her later to see what people have been telling her at the bakery."

Emily nodded. "Trish is the gossip queen of Oak Hill. If anyone spotted Tessa around town yesterday, she would hear about it eventually."

Emily and Clint both sipped their coffee in silence for a few moments, then Emily said hesitantly, "Clint, I have a favor to ask. I know you and Kelly are getting to be friends, and I wonder if you would talk to her about Scott today. Kelly says he's hiding somewhere, because the entity that killed him has followed him here to Eternal Rest. But if he's not here, I can't help him. Can you please ask Kelly if she can talk Scott into coming home?"

"Of course," Clint answered without hesitation. "You know I'm happy to help."

Emily wondered if Clint's eagerness was because he really did want to help Scott or because it was just another excuse for him to communicate with Kelly. Both, Emily decided. It was a strange relationship, but Clint didn't seem to mind that Kelly was a ghost.

When the doorbell rang, Emily once again felt hope rising in her. She couldn't hide her disappointment when she opened the door to see it was just Steven. He had dark circles under his bloodshot eyes.

"No news, I assume?" he asked her.

"None. Come on in. Breakfast is still out. Help yourself."

Clint was already seated at Emily's desk, so Emily grabbed her feather duster and began working her way through the parlor. She could hear Steven and her guests talking quietly in the dining room, and she knew her own feelings about Tessa's disappearance were nothing in comparison with theirs. Tessa was simply Emily's guest. To the others, she was so much more.

Suddenly, Rylee's voice rose angrily. "Are you serious? Are we supposed to pretend nothing is wrong?"

"I don't know what else to do!" Steven's voice was nearly as loud, but it sounded more exasperated than angry. "We can't afford to get behind schedule. You're going to have to step up until Tessa is back."

"When we find Tessa, she is going to rip your head off," Vic said. "She does not like to be upstaged."

"Then she shouldn't have gone missing, should she?" Steven countered.

Emily wasn't trying to eavesdrop, but it was impossible not to hear every word of the heated conversation. She had thought Steven's obvious lack of sleep had been due to his worrying about Tessa, but at the moment, Emily wondered if he was more stressed out about his TV show.

Brian finally spoke up, his voice quiet but firm. "I think we should be focused on finding Tessa, not on trying to film her own show without her."

"For once, you and I agree on something," Vic said icily.

The conversation quieted after that, and Emily could no longer hear what was being said. She had given up dusting and was standing just to the side of the parlor doorway, listening. Even Clint had turned around in his chair, staring in the direction of the dining room with his mouth agape. When he caught Emily's eye, he mouthed, "Drama!"

Emily just nodded and returned to her housework. She was on the front porch, attempting to sand down a rough spot in one of the floorboards, when Steven and her guests trooped out the door. Emily stood up warily, unsure what to say.

"Steven and I are going to do some filming today," Rylee said. She sounded hesitant, almost timid. "You know, just generic footage we can work into the episode."

"And Vic and I are going to keep searching the town," Brian said. He shook his head, and as he began to walk down the porch steps, Emily overhead him mutter to himself, "This is not how this week was supposed to go."

Emily was once again on her hands and knees, sanding away at the wooden board, when her phone rang. She knew before she even pulled it out of the back pocket of her black jeans that it was Danny, and she rushed to answer it.

"We haven't found her yet, but we did talk to a couple of folks who were working at Under the Covers yesterday," Danny began. "Would you like to come to the station? They gave us some interesting details, but I can't figure out if they're important to this case or not. I think having a fresh pair of eyes looking at the information might help."

Danny had been trying to keep Emily out of investigations lately, worried she would put herself in danger, so Emily was pleased he was inviting her to participate in this one. "I'm on my way," she told him.

The Oak Hill Police Department had been in the same two-story brick building for nearly a century. It was near the downtown square, and Emily promised herself she would walk that way later to get lunch from The Depot.

Danny's face was grim when Emily was ushered into his office at the back of the ground floor. "We tried finding her by tracking her cell phone," Danny began, shutting the door to his office as Emily sat down. "No luck: an employee at the bookshop found it stashed there."

"Stashed?" Emily asked, confused.

"Several books had been pulled away from the shelf,

and the phone was behind them, completely hidden," Danny explained. "The employee only found it because he noticed the book spines were sticking out too far, and when he tried to push the books back into place, they wouldn't budge."

"Do you think Tessa left it there, or did someone make her do it?" All kinds of new, dark possibilities were popping up in Emily's mind.

Danny sighed. "We just don't know yet. There were two employees working at the shop when Tessa came in yesterday afternoon, shortly after three. That matches what Sage told us. She was in there for nearly an hour, and she was mostly in the history section."

"Maybe she was looking up Oak Hill history books to get ideas about where else to film," Emily suggested.

"You would think so, but she didn't put away several of the books she was looking at. They were just laid on top of the shelved books. Here." Danny grabbed a stack of books from his desk and handed them to Emily.

Emily frowned as she read the titles of the three books. "*Fashion Through the Ages*, *Quack Cures and Snake-Oil Salesmen*, and *To Lead with Purpose: Notable Figures of the 19th Century*. I don't get it. What do any of these have to do with Oak Hill history?"

"Perhaps Tessa wasn't doing research for the TV show at all," Danny suggested. "She may have simply been perusing books."

Emily narrowed her eyes. "She cut out of Monday's filming early without telling anyone she was leaving, all so she could do a little shopping? Speaking of which, did she actually buy anything?"

"A sparkling water and a cinnamon roll at the shop's coffee bar."

"None of this helps us."

"It at least lets us know that as of approximately four

o'clock yesterday afternoon, Tessa Valentine was alive and well. The employees said she turned left out of the shop—they only took note because they recognized her and were too nosy not to keep an eye on her—so Roger and a couple other officers are going along that side of the street to see if she was seen anywhere else."

Emily ran a hand over the top book in the stack. "Did anyone mention if Tessa was acting strangely before she disappeared yesterday? Maybe going to the bookshop was just an excuse to get away from someone in her group."

"You think maybe she got in a fight with someone or felt threatened?"

"Maybe, though I can't imagine she would stay away so long, if that were the case. From what I saw of her, she relishes conflict because it gets her attention. She was actually excited about the protesters yesterday morning."

"Protesters, yes…" Danny said slowly. His eyes fixed on something over Emily's shoulder.

"What about them?" Emily prompted.

"They were obviously keeping tabs on her. Maybe one of them knows where she went."

"Roger sent them all home."

"From your house, yes, but that doesn't mean they weren't waiting to wave their signs in front of Tessa elsewhere." Danny leaned forward and began scribbling notes on his notepad.

While Danny wrote, Emily began idly flipping through the pages of the book about quack cures. She was just a short way into the book when a small piece of paper fluttered to the ground. It had fallen out of the book. Emily reached down to grab it, but Danny must have noticed her movement, because he half-stood as he shouted, "Don't touch it!"

Emily froze, her fingers just inches from the paper, and

looked up at Danny with surprise. "Why not? Oh! It might be evidence, right? There might be fingerprints on it."

"Exactly." Already, Danny was pulling a pair of rubber gloves out of his desk drawer. He slipped them on, then came around to Emily's side of the desk and gingerly picked up the note. It was no bigger than an index card, and someone had written on it in capital letters, *If you tell, I tell. The world will know you're a fraud.*

"So somebody was threatening Tessa," Emily said, reading over Danny's shoulder.

"It sounds like someone was trying to keep her quiet about something, but who? And about what?" Danny frowned. "Also, why did Tessa leave the note in a book? She must have wanted us to find it, but I can't imagine how it's going to help *us* find *her*."

Emily's phone began to ring, and she pulled it out of her purse to see it was Sage calling. "Hey, Sage."

"Em," Sage began, her voice quieter than Emily had ever heard it.

Emily sat up straight, instantly concerned. "What's wrong?" She saw Danny's hand freeze, the note dangling from his fingertips as he looked up at her, his face tight.

"I think I'm in trouble," Sage finally said. "I came to the shop to do a little cleaning, and Tessa is here."

"Oh, thank goodness." Emily breathed a sigh of relief.

"She's dead."

10

Emily was still trying to process what Sage had just said when someone burst into Danny's office. "We gotta go!" a man shouted behind her. At the same time, Sage said, "I just called nine one one."

Danny was already up and moving around his desk, sparing just a split second to look at Emily. From his expression, she knew he had figured out the only thing that could be so urgent.

"The police are on their way, Sage," Emily mumbled into the phone. Seeing Beyond was just a few blocks away from the police station, and they would be there in a matter of minutes.

"You're coming, too, right?" Sage's voice began to rise in both volume and pitch. "Em, I need you. There's a dead woman in my office. A woman who I have been very open about not liking. This does not look good for me."

"I'm walking over there right now. Sit tight, Sage." Emily put her phone down and stared blankly at the wall behind Danny's desk. She wasn't seeing the map of Oak Hill pinned there or the many sticky notes he had put up. Instead, she was picturing the expressions on her guests' faces when they found out the news. She hoped fervently that Danny or Roger or anyone but her, really, would be the one to tell them the news. Emily did not want that burden.

Emily stood slowly, feeling like her limbs were trying to move through molasses. She leaned forward and rested her hands on Danny's desk, taking a few deep breaths as she steeled herself for whatever she was about to walk into.

On her way out of the police station, Emily heard Tessa's name at least three times. The entire station was buzzing with the news.

There was a police car blocking each end of the stretch of street on which Sage's office building sat. The two-story Art Deco building usually looked bright and charming with its white plaster facade, but on that day, it managed to take on an ominous look.

Already, a small crowd of people had gathered behind each of the police cars and on the sidewalk across the street. Emily heard a shout and looked up to see the same woman who had been protesting outside her house only the day before. She didn't have a sign with her, yet all eyes were on her as she shouted about justice being served.

The woman turned in Emily's direction, and Emily quickly averted her gaze, but it was too late. The woman pointed at her and yelled, "You see! I knew having that evil woman in Oak Hill would cause trouble. You housed her. You helped her. You brought this plague on our town!"

Emily clamped her teeth together and continued walking, keeping her eyes on the front door of the building. Roger Newton was stationed at the door. His stocky body seemed like even more of a barrier with his arms crossed and his shoulders squared, and he eyed Emily doubtfully. "Miss Emily, this is a crime scene," he warned.

"Sage needs me," Emily pleaded.

Roger glanced toward the protester, who was still shouting, then back to Emily. "Don't touch anything," he said, turning just enough that Emily could slip past him.

Emily sprinted up the stairs. When she came out of the stairwell onto the second floor, she found the hallway crowded with police officers, EMTs, and even two firemen. She picked her way among the people until she reached the door of Seeing Beyond, which was propped open. There were fewer people inside, and an officer was already putting up crime scene tape. It started at Sage's giant oak desk and went around the back of the midnight-blue velvet sofa in the middle of the room, and then across to the edge of the bookcases Sage had arranged in a U-shape. Inside was a cozy, private little spot where Sage communicated with the dead for her customers.

Or she did, at least, before she had lost her mediumship abilities.

The dark-toned throw rugs Sage had put all over the room—nearly obscuring the boring, beige office carpeting—muffled the noise in the room slightly. There were several conversations happening as well as the *click-click* of someone taking photos and a cell phone ringing with a jaunty tune that seemed wildly out of place in such a situation. Emily could see Sage standing near her desk, her head down and her shoulders slumped. Her wife, Jen, was standing next to her, an arm around Sage's shoulders and her body turned just slightly to create a bit of a barrier between Sage and the crime scene. Whatever Jen was saying to Sage was lost in the buzz of voices.

As she got closer, Emily heard Jen say, "Emily is here." In answer, Sage just lifted a hand, her fingers groping for Emily's. Emily held her best friend's hand tightly as she grit her teeth and looked over her shoulder. From the doorway, she hadn't been able to see Tessa's body. From this position, though, Emily could see her lying face down on the rug in front of the sofa. Emily quickly turned back to Sage.

"Why was she in my shop, Em?" Sage asked. From the

sound, Emily could tell she had been crying. "How did she even get in the door? I'm certain it was locked!"

"We'll find out, Sage. It's going to be okay."

"Not if I'm a murder suspect!" Sage's outburst was so loud that the din of voices behind Emily quieted for a moment.

"No one is accusing you of murder," Jen said soothingly. "Besides, we don't even know if she was murdered."

Sage finally raised her head, her cheeks streaked with tears and her eyes red. "Oh, sure," she said sarcastically. "She just broke into my office and dropped dead of natural causes."

"How did she die?" Emily asked.

Sage gave a little shrug. "No idea. I walked in, and there she was, face down on my rug. I haven't found even a drop of blood. Her clothes are clean, too. At least, what I can see of them."

"No signs of a struggle, then," Emily surmised.

"Exactly."

Emily's mind went back to her earlier thought that Tessa had called Sage to pick her up not because she had a sudden urge to go book shopping, but because she had been trying to extract herself from her situation or from someone specific. The note Tessa had stashed in the book certainly seemed to confirm the theory she was being threatened by someone.

"She called you for a ride yesterday," Emily said. "Maybe she came here trying to find you again."

"But for what?" Jen asked. "Tessa's name is like a swear word in our house."

"I think she needed help, and she didn't know who else to turn to." For all of Tessa's notoriety, Emily reflected, and all the people who professed to adore her, it was sad to think she might have felt like going to an enemy for help was her only recourse. Or…

"Or she was planted here to make me look guilty," Sage said bitterly.

Emily raised her eyebrows. "I think your abilities are beginning to come back, because I was just thinking the exact same thing. When I was at the police station, Danny let me look at some books Tessa had left out at Under the Covers, almost like she wanted us to get some kind of secret message from them. In fact, we did sort of find a secret message. A note was in one of the books, threatening Tessa that if she spoke up about something, then the writer of the note would expose her as a fraudulent medium. It's possible the note was written by her killer. If Tessa knew a secret about them, maybe they got tired of threatening her to stay quiet and jumped straight to murder."

"And I haven't tried to keep my opinion of Tessa to myself," Sage said nervously. "If someone wanted an easy target to pin her murder on, it would certainly be me."

"Oh, Emily, how nice to see you," interrupted a friendly voice. Emily turned to see J.D. Bonim, Jr., the owner of J.D. Bonim and Sons Funeral Home. J.D. bustled over, his smile looking out of place in the middle of a crime scene. His wire-rimmed glasses and navy-blue suit made him stand out even more. He was, by far, the best-dressed person in the room.

"J.D., hello. I take it you're here to, ah…" Emily faltered.

"I'm working with the coroner, yes," J.D. supplied. "Your guests don't have a very good track record lately. Goodness."

"Not lately."

"I sure hope Ms. Valentine's ghost has stuck around to let you know how she wound up in this position!" J.D. said, winking.

"Us, too," Emily agreed. "Rest assured, we'll be trying to establish contact once things have quieted down here."

"*You'll* be trying," Sage said under her breath.

"I'll leave you ladies to it. Have a nice afternoon." J.D. nodded around at the three of them, then returned to the police and medical personnel who were clustered near the sofa.

"Have a nice afternoon?" Jen repeated incredulously. "Does he think we're at a Chamber of Commerce mixer?"

"I've noticed J.D. tends to have a casual attitude when it comes to dead bodies," Emily said.

"You're right that we need to wait until later if we're going to have a conversation with Tessa's ghost," Sage said, "if she's even here. Emily, can you sense anything? Still your mind, and try to let all the other noise fade into the background."

Emily closed her eyes and tried to imagine her consciousness physically expanding in a widening halo that grew from just around her head to every corner of the room. She breathed deeply, and after a few moments, the individual voices she could hear began to merge into a sort of hum.

"Tessa?" Emily whispered. "Are you here?"

Emily heard a faint noise, almost like a tapping sound, but she wasn't sure if it was paranormal or just the movement of the first responders behind her.

"Tessa, if you are here with us, please give us a sign." Emily furrowed her brow in concentration.

There was a loud bang behind Emily, and she whirled around.

"That was just somebody dropping their medical case," Sage said. "They'd better not mess up my rugs."

Emily felt a little rattled, and she tried to shake it off as she closed her eyes again. "Tessa, we know there's a good chance your spirit is still here. We want to help you," she said quietly yet urgently. "Please, if you are here, let us know. You're a psychic medium. You know how all of this works."

"To be fair," Sage interjected, "she doesn't know how it works from the other side. It might take her a minute to figure it out. She was a hack medium, so maybe she'll be a hack ghost, too."

Emily opened her eyes just in time to see a book fly off the shelf behind Sage and Jen. "Look out!" Emily cried.

11

Sage and Jen both instinctively ducked as the book sailed between them and landed on the floor right in front of Sage. The book was open, and Sage bent at the waist to read it. She stood up and began to laugh heartily.

Jen gave Sage a little nudge. "People are watching," she said nervously. "You probably shouldn't laugh when the police are trying to figure out why there's a dead lady in your shop."

"Oh, right," Sage said, looking over at the other people in the room but not seeming at all embarrassed about her outburst. "I guess I don't want them to think I'm gloating over my kill."

"Sage!" Jen and Emily hissed at the same time.

Sage waved off their protests and pointed down at the book. It had opened to the start of a chapter. "*Discerning Authenticity from Fraud*," Sage read. "Tessa is definitely here, and I don't think she liked my comment about her being a hack."

As if in answer, there was another of the thumping sounds Emily had heard earlier. This time, it was clear the sound was coming from the bookcase behind Jen and Sage. Emily could see a large hardback book vibrating so strongly it was banging against the bookcase.

"Okay, I'm sorry I called you a hack!" Sage said in an exasperated tone.

The noise stopped immediately.

"Em, tell her we'll be back for a more meaningful conversation, just as soon as everyone has cleared out."

"I expect she heard you just fine," Emily answered. Still, she reiterated Sage's promise that they would attempt to communicate with Tessa later.

Emily felt a hand on her back and turned to see Danny. "Sorry to interrupt, ladies. Sage, let's go down to the station, where it's quieter. I need to know every single detail of your interaction with Tessa yesterday as well as your discovery this morning."

"Of course," Sage said soberly.

"I'm coming with you," Jen said, gripping Sage's hand tightly.

Danny turned to Emily. "Roger is already on his way to Eternal Rest to inform your guests of the news."

"They're not there. Steven wanted to get more filming done, so Rylee is out doing that with him and the crew. Brian and Vic said they wanted to keep looking for Tessa."

"They've actually been filming this morning? While the star of the show was missing?" Danny looked horrified. "I didn't know producers were so ruthless."

"To be fair, I don't think Steven knew what else to do," Emily said, though she also thought it seemed like a heartless move.

"Roger will round them all up and break the news. How about you? Will you be okay?" Danny was looking at Emily with the intensity she had seen in his eyes a few times before.

"Another one of my guests is dead," Emily said flatly. "Right now, though, Sage and my still-living guests are more important than me. I barely knew her."

Danny hesitated, then nodded. "Okay. I'll call you later to see how you're doing."

"Thanks."

Danny, Sage, and Jen left while Emily picked up the book Tessa had thrown to the floor. She found its spot on the shelf and replaced it while whispering, "Thanks for the sign, Tessa. Talk to you soon."

Emily turned around and realized it was just her and a lot of police and medical personnel she didn't know in the room. With the exception, of course, of J.D., who was having what looked like a pleasant conversation with someone, despite the fact there was a dead body at his feet.

Emily quickly turned her head away from the scene in front of the sofa. One of her guests was dead, the dark entity had found its way to Eternal Rest, and Scott's ghost was hiding somewhere, afraid to come back home. Nothing was going the way it was supposed to. Emily felt tears welling in her eyes, and she made as quick of an exit as she could from Seeing Beyond. She paused in the stairwell, willing herself not to cry.

You can cry later. Don't let that protester see how upset you are.

Emily hitched her purse higher on her shoulder and walked out of the building, her head held high in defiance of everything she was feeling.

That bravery crumbled as soon as Emily saw how big the crowd had grown. At least fifty people were standing in the street, many of them holding up cell phones to take video or pictures. Emily was suddenly struck with how detrimental this could be for Sage. It was bad enough she had lost her psychic mediumship abilities, but looking like a possible murder suspect was far worse. Oak Hill loved a good scandal, and in a community where many already eyed psychics with distrust, it might be hard for Sage to keep Seeing Beyond afloat, even if her abilities came back. The backlash from this could drive her out of business.

Tears stung Emily's eyes again, and the sea of faces blurred. She turned right on the sidewalk, not caring where she was going as long as she got out of there quickly. Her gaze was directed down at the sidewalk, so she could avoid meeting the eyes of all the people she knew were watching.

Emily took two strides and saw someone step right in front of her. Defiantly, Emily plowed forward as she raised her head, her chin jutting out. It was only before running right into the person that she realized it was Trevor. Instead of stopping to avoid the collision, she took another step forward and wrapped her arms around him. She hid her face in his chest as she began to cry.

One of Trevor's hands gently cradled the back of Emily's head as he hugged her tightly. Finally, as Emily's tears began to slow, he said quietly, "Want to go hide from the world for a little bit?"

"Yes, please," Emily said in a cracked voice.

Trevor turned so he stood between Emily and all the people crowded in the street. He kept one arm around her shoulders as he steered her a short distance away, where his car was parked. The second Emily was seated in the car and the door was closed, she breathed out a sigh of relief. It was nice to have a physical barrier between herself and the chaos at Seeing Beyond.

As Trevor guided the car out of the parking spot and onto the road leading away from Sage's office building and downtown Oak Hill, he said, "I was actually going to check on Sage. I didn't expect to see you there."

"She had just left with Danny before you ran into me."

"*You* ran into *me*," Trevor said teasingly, then his tone turned serious. "When you say Sage left with Danny…"

"Just to give a statement. We don't even know how Tessa died yet, let alone whether it was murder."

Trevor glanced at Emily with his blue eyes. "Do you think it was murder?"

"I think it's likely. We found a threatening note someone sent to Tessa. Apparently, she knew something she wasn't supposed to. Plus, Sage's office was locked, Trevor. I think someone broke in there to frame Sage for murder."

"That means someone either killed Tessa, then hauled her body into the building, or they lured her there to kill her on site."

"The second option is the most likely, of course. I just don't know who would have such a big grudge against Sage that they would frame her for murder."

"You're making a big assumption," Trevor pointed out. They were at a stop sign, and he turned right onto a two-lane road leading toward the rolling hills northeast of Oak Hill. "Sage is a psychic medium. Tessa was a psychic medium. If I had killed Tessa and wanted to cover it up, Sage would definitely be on my short list of people to frame for it, whether or not I had something against her."

"Good point. This may not be about making Sage look bad, but about keeping the focus away from the real killer."

"If it was, in fact, a murder."

"Right." Emily turned her attention to the trees they were speeding past. The green leaves looked wilted and sun-weary.

After another few minutes, Trevor rounded a curve and began to slow down. "The drive is somewhere along here. There it is!" He turned left onto a narrow dirt path that plunged into the trees.

"Where are we going?" Emily finally asked.

"To a place I used to come after my brother went missing. Everyone at school was talking about Dylan's disappearance, then I would go home, and my mom and sister would be talking about it. My dad would get angry at every little thing. I had to find a place where I could get a break from it all."

The path made a sharp right turn, then ended abruptly in front of a pair of crumbling granite pillars that stood about eight feet high. One of them was leaning at a dangerous angle, and a rusted iron gate stood haphazardly between the columns, still connected only by the bottom hinge.

"Welcome to the secret cemetery," Trevor said.

"I can't believe you haven't told me about this place," Emily said distractedly. She was already climbing out of the car as she spoke.

Beyond the pillars and the gate, Emily could see the tops of old headstones floating in a sea of weeds. There was no point trying to get through the broken gate since the iron fence around the cemetery had crumbled to the ground. Emily stepped over its remains and began to wade through the weeds, which came up past her knees in some places. She headed right for the nearest headstone, which had turned nearly black with dirt and neglect.

"There's no engraving on this one," she called to Trevor.

"There's no engraving on any of them," he answered.

Emily turned. "Why not?"

"Your guess is as good as mine. There are only fifteen or twenty graves here. An old family cemetery, I suppose." Trevor stepped up next to Emily. "One of the early settlers of Oak Hill must have lived near here."

Emily gazed around at the trees that closed them in. "The stone monuments have outlived what was probably a wooden house," she said, fascinated. "I wonder if there are ghosts here."

"Only one way to find out," Trevor answered.

Emily shook her head. "I can't even communicate with Scott, let alone a bunch of strangers in a secret cemetery."

Trevor gave Emily a searching look. "You were upset when you came out of Sage's shop today, but it wasn't just about Tessa, was it? Come on. There's a big boulder over there under that oak tree. We can sit on it while you tell me everything that's going on."

The weeds were less tall and thick under the oak tree, and when Emily sat down on the boulder, she could feel the chill of the stone through her jeans. Between that and the shade of the tree, she couldn't imagine a cooler spot on such a hot day. "I see why you used to come here," she told Trevor.

"You need this place, too, obviously. I'm sorry Tessa wasn't just missing. When I heard one of my co-workers gossiping about a dead body being found, I knew it was Tessa before she even said it."

"Poor Sage. What a shock it must have been for her to walk into her shop and see Tessa lying there like that." From there, Emily poured her heart out to Trevor, telling him not just everything that had happened at Sage's that day, but also her frustration about the entity standing between her and Scott. She concluded with, "There are so many things that need to be made right, and I just feel helpless."

"You're not helpless, Emily. If you can't have a talk with Scott right now, then maybe you should talk to the entity," Trevor suggested.

"Even if it is just the ghost of a girl, like Rylee thinks, it could be dangerous because it's so angry at me." Emily felt a chill run up her back at the idea of trying to have a conversation with something so malicious.

"We'll all come support you if you decide to do it," Trevor said. "And, don't forget, you've already established contact with Tessa's ghost, and you're going to go back for more. My point is, you're not helpless. You can talk to these ghosts—"

"I can't communicate with them the way Sage can," Emily protested.

"Yes, you can, Emily. Look how much you communicated with Helen Harper's ghost. You should believe in yourself. The more you do, the better you'll become."

Emily stood up abruptly. "You weren't there at the séance Saturday night. I couldn't control the conversation, and that entity showed up and tried to shake my house down! While you were out having a nice dinner, I was trying to keep my guests from panicking." She hadn't intended the words to come out so bitingly, and Trevor jerked backward, a look of hurt on his face. Emily's shoulders sank, and she dropped her head. "I'm sorry. I'm not angry at you, Trevor. I'm just frustrated and overwhelmed. I should go home. I need to be there for my guests."

Trevor led the way back to his car, and he didn't say anything until he dropped Emily off in front of her car at the police station. "I believe in you, Emily. You should, too," was all he said.

Emily felt even more miserable than before as she drove home. Her heart lightened for a moment when she turned into her driveway and saw Trish walking up the front porch steps with her delivery of baked goods. Emily stopped her car at the bottom of the porch and got out, and her spirits sank again as Trish turned to her with mascara-streaked cheeks.

"Can you believe Tessa is dead, Emily?" Trish sniffed loudly. "If I had known she was going to keel over, I would have asked her for an autograph when she came into my bakery yesterday afternoon."

12

Emily flew up the porch steps and grasped Trish by the shoulders. "Tessa was at Grainy Day? When?"

Trish looked startled. "Yesterday afternoon, like I just said."

"What time?"

Trish took a few hesitant steps backward, until she was out of Emily's reach. She held up the bags of baked goods like a shield. "Maybe around four or so. Why? What's going on?"

Emily realized her arms were still reaching forward, and she dropped them self-consciously. "Sorry, Trish. I'm just really on edge. First that stupid dark entity shows up to get between me and Scott, then Tessa turns up dead in Sage's waiting room, and then I was mean to Trevor just now, even though he was only trying to help me…"

Awareness came into Trish's eyes. "Oh," she said softly, drawing out the word. "My hands are full, but you're going to open this door, march straight to your kitchen, and pour us each a glass of wine. And then I'll tell you every little detail I can remember about Tessa's visit, just as soon as you tell me why it's important."

Trish had heard about Tessa's body being found at Seeing Beyond, like most of Oak Hill surely had already, but the fact Tessa had been missing the previous afternoon hadn't reached her ears yet.

"I'm surprised," Emily said when Trish confessed her ignorance of it. She filled the wine glasses she had placed on the kitchen table. "I would have figured the whole town knew by now."

"Folks were probably so busy gossiping about where her body turned up that they forgot to mention she had gone missing for a while." Trish shrugged, then took a long sip of wine. "I guess it was a little after four when Tessa came in. I was already starting to prep the next day's dough. She said she had just been at Under the Covers and decided to pop in for something to eat. She said she had a terrible headache, and she hoped a little sugar might do her good."

Emily frowned. "She had a cinnamon roll at the bookshop. I'm surprised she was hungry again so soon."

"She ordered a couple of biscuits and a lemon bar. I threw in a slice of my peach tart for her, like I'd promised. I put everything in a box, and then she headed out."

"Which direction did she go?"

"She turned right out of the bakery." Trish gasped quietly. "In the direction of Seeing Beyond. Oh, no, Emily, do you think I'm the last one who saw her alive? Do you think my biscuits killed her?"

Emily put up a hand. "No, Trish, I don't think your biscuits were involved this time around." *At least, I hope not,* Emily added silently. "Did she say anything other than that she had a headache?"

"Just a little small talk. How hot it was, that they had gotten some really good footage at the mill for the TV show, how worn out she was. That sort of thing. Honestly, she seemed a little off to me. I had figured that charm she gave me when I met her here the other day was just a persona, but whatever I expected the genuine

Tessa Valentine to be like, it wasn't what I met yesterday."

"In real life, she was a diva," Emily said. "I hate to speak ill of the dead, but it's the truth."

"What I saw yesterday wasn't a diva, and it was more than just the headache making her act differently," Trish said confidently. "She seemed a bit out of sorts. Distracted."

"Interesting. Sage also sensed there was something off about Tessa yesterday. I'm sure Danny is going to want to know everything you just told me. It will help them piece together the timeline from Tessa leaving the bookstore to her showing up dead at Seeing Beyond."

"Isn't there some other hot detective I could talk to?" Trish grumbled. "I still haven't forgiven Detective Hernandez for suspecting me in Thornton Daley's murder."

"Thornton was poisoned with your biscuits," Emily pointed out.

"I know, and both his death and his ghost have been great for business," Trish said grudgingly. "Fine, I'll call him. But first—" Trish grabbed the wine bottle and topped off her glass.

Emily's guests returned to Eternal Rest shortly after Trish had left. They were all understandably subdued, and Emily gave them her quiet condolences. It was only seven o'clock, but Vic, Rylee, and Brian all went upstairs and into their rooms, where they stayed for the rest of the night. Emily thought about going up to see if they wanted anything to eat for dinner, then decided to let them mourn in peace.

When Emily put breakfast out on Wednesday morning, she expected her guests wouldn't actually come down to eat it. She was surprised, then, when Vic and Rylee came downstairs at exactly eight o'clock. When Emily asked them how they were doing, Rylee shrugged sadly. "I think I'm still in shock. The place where they found Tessa, that's your friend's shop, right? The woman Steven and I met at the séance."

"Sage, yes."

"How did Tessa wind up there? I thought they didn't like each other."

"They didn't," Emily admitted. "We're not sure why Tessa went to Seeing Beyond or how she got inside."

Rylee swallowed hard. "If you don't mind, I'd like to go there. I want to see where she... I want to see if I get any psychic impressions."

"Not yet," Vic said firmly. "You're still too upset. Take some time first."

Rylee just nodded and stared into her coffee cup.

Brian was coming downstairs as Emily was exiting the dining room, and unlike his companions, he looked more angry than sad. Emily glanced over her shoulder just in time to see him flop down in a chair with a huff.

At nine, Rylee found Emily in the parlor to tell her they were heading out for the day.

"Oh," Emily said, surprised. "Are you going to the funeral home?"

"No," Rylee said, seeming just as surprised that Emily would even suggest such a thing. "We're filming again. Now that we know Tessa, um, won't be coming back, Steven is going to make me the star of the show. We've got a lot of work to do today."

"Oh," Emily said again. She wasn't sure what else to say. "Congratulations on getting the dead woman's starring role" didn't seem appropriate.

Rylee suddenly laughed self-consciously, and she ran a hand across her forehead, leaving her bangs askew. "I know. It's completely ridiculous, isn't it? Hours after Tessa is found, and suddenly Steven is sticking me in the spotlight. I'm not ready for this. I'm not as good as Tessa was."

Vic appeared behind Rylee, and he put a comforting hand on her shoulder. "You're every bit as talented as Tessa," he said. "You just have to believe in yourself."

Emily smiled to herself since Trevor had said those same words to her.

"I know," Rylee said. "Throwing me into the top spot will give me more experience, and more experience helps me grow as a medium."

"Exactly. Tessa would be proud to hear you looking at it like that."

Rylee snorted. "She'd be furious that I'm taking her spot."

"That, too," Vic agreed. "Come on, let's go. We'll see you this evening, Emily."

Even Brian left, and Emily figured he didn't want to drive home yet, but he didn't want to sit around Eternal Rest all day, either. With the house to herself, Emily cleaned the dining room and the guest rooms. She tried reaching out to Scott, too, but there was no response, and she figured he was still hiding from the dark entity.

Sage and Emily had made plans to meet at Seeing Beyond at eleven o'clock. Sage had said it would give Emily time to do her tasks around Eternal Rest first, and it would have them wrapping up their séance with Tessa just in time for lunch at The Depot.

When Emily arrived at the building where Seeing Beyond was located, she was happy to see there wasn't a crowd outside again. There was no sign that it had been the focus of the entire town's attention only a day before. It was just an ordinary office building.

Seeing Beyond, however, was a different story. There was still police tape blocking off the rug in front of the sofa, and Emily found Sage sitting at her desk, staring at the area with distaste.

"I'm going to have to throw that rug out and get a new one," Sage said in greeting.

"Why, is there blood on it?" Emily stepped up to the police tape and peered at the rug, but it didn't look any different to her.

"Not a drop. Tessa's death was neat and tidy, at least. Still, you know I get a little squeamish about bodies."

"I know. How are you doing today?"

Sage stood and joined Emily at the edge of the tape. "My phone has been ringing off the hook. People don't care that I can't connect them with their dead loved ones. They're asking for lessons on how to do it themselves, they're booking consultations for Tarot card readings—I don't even offer that, but I said yes! People want to be here, at the heart of the scandal."

"It's a weird reason for them to be booking sessions with you," Emily agreed, turning to Sage, "but I like where this is going. Until your abilities return, teaching others how to tap into their own sixth sense is a great way to keep your business going."

"It had never occurred to me there would be so much interest in that. This could save my checking account, Em."

"And I'm happy people aren't avoiding your business because of this," Emily added.

"There was a protester outside this morning," Sage said, almost proudly.

"Let me guess: long brown hair in a braid, loud voice?"

"Yeah. She comes around now and then. She never stays long, because the other tenants here talk her into leaving."

"She was at my house the other day, protesting Tessa."

"Lucky you! Welcome to the Oak Hill Society of Outcasts."

There was a thunk behind Emily and Sage, and they both whirled around. A book was lying on the rug in front of the bookcase. "Yes, Tessa," Sage called impatiently. "We haven't forgotten you. Let's do this!"

Sage ducked under the police tape and walked to the bookcases arranged in a U-shape along one wall. She gave the rug where Tessa had been found a wide berth, skirting along the edges of the area to reach the curtained entrance to the space inside the bookcases. Sage pulled aside the beaded curtain, then turned and waved at Emily to follow.

Emily had seen the consultation area, but she had never actually sat down in it. It was just large enough for a small round table and four chairs. The table was covered in a dark red cloth, and Sage's séance instruments were already arranged on it: a purple seven-day candle, a bell, a silver dollar, a few pieces of blank paper, and a pencil. Sage had draped what looked like scarves between the upper shelves of the bookcases, forming a sort of ceiling over the space. The scarves were dark, mostly shades of red and blue in a paisley pattern. Between the scarves overhead, the curtain at the entrance, and the books cramming the shelves, it was dim and almost spooky inside. Emily knew Sage did it partly for ambiance but also for practicality: if a ghost manipulated the candle flame or, even better, actually appeared to Sage and her customers, it was easier to see it in the dim light rather than the glare of the overhead office lights.

Emily sat down opposite Sage, who reached forward and took Emily's hands in her own. "You can do this," she said. "Tessa is clearly eager to communicate."

Emily gripped Sage's fingers and shut her eyes. "Tessa Valentine, Sage and I are ready to communicate with you again. We want to help you. Can you give us a sign that you're here?"

As Emily listened hard for an answer, she realized one of her fingers was tapping rapidly against Sage's. "Sorry," she whispered apologetically. Emily opened her eyes and stared at her hand. "I can't stop it. It's like I have a nervous tick."

Sage grinned at Emily. "It's Tessa! She wants to do automatic writing through you!" Sage dropped Emily's hands and pushed the paper toward her. "Take the pencil, and relax your hand. Try to relax your gaze, too, so you're not reading as she's writing. It's best to be as passive as possible."

Emily did as Sage instructed, holding the pencil over the paper as loosely as she could. She gasped when her hand began to move of its own accord, and Sage had to remind her to relax and focus.

After about a minute, Emily's hand stopped moving. She dropped the pencil and flexed her fingers. "I think she's done," Emily said. She leaned forward and read what Tessa had written through her out loud. "*I said you were a fraud, and here you are, having to bring in someone else to communicate with me.*"

"That stings," Sage mumbled angrily.

"Of all the things to communicate," Emily said, disgusted. She had thought she wanted to help Tessa's ghost, but she was suddenly having second thoughts.

Sage huffed out a breath. "I guess it's time for me to come clean about my history with Tessa, and why we dislike each other so much."

"You remember I used to do about half a dozen psychic fairs every year?" Sage began. When Emily nodded, she continued, "At the fairs, you get your own little booth, and attendees who are interested in your services can consult with you right then and there. Tessa usually had a booth, too. She wasn't a big celebrity psychic back then, even though she acted like it. Tessa and I weren't friends—her ego was too big for my taste—but we certainly weren't enemies. At least, not until the fair in Charlotte four years ago." Sage paused and pursed her lips.

"What happened?" Emily prompted.

"The organizers of the fair set up a special after-hours event. For an extra fee, attendees could join a couple of mediums for a walk through a haunted place. They asked me to be one of the mediums, and they offered me a nice chunk of money to do it, so I said yes. I didn't realize until the day of the event that Tessa would be the other medium participating."

"Uh-oh."

"Yeah. We were at an old mansion about half an hour outside of Charlotte, in the middle of the woods. I could tell as soon as we walked in that there were about four ghosts there, two of them particularly strong. The plan was for us to split up: Tessa and I would each take about ten people and lead them around, giving our impressions of the ghosts as we explored the mansion. Before we could do that, though, Tessa started shouting about how full the house was of ghosts. She claimed she was seeing them everywhere, and true to her style, they all looked tortured and miserable. It was a real spectacle."

Emily rolled her eyes. "It sounds a lot like what happened at my house."

"Well, you know me. I called her out on it. I accused her of making claims that weren't true, and she started shouting at me, calling me jealous and a fake. She said if I was a true psychic medium, I'd be able to sense all of those ghosts, too. I lost my temper and started shouting back at her. Eventually, the person from the fair who was coordinating the evening pulled us both aside. Tessa insisted that I leave, and since she was starting to get more notoriety by that point, the fair organizer sided with her. I was so embarrassed that I didn't even return to the fair the next day. I just went home."

"Was that the last time you and Tessa ever spoke?" Emily asked.

"It was. I stopped doing psychic fairs after that, partly because I was still so embarrassed but mostly because I didn't want to run into her. Of course, she used my absence to her advantage, telling everyone that it proved her point. I was a fraud who was afraid to show my face again, according to her."

"Wow, Sage. I had no idea it was that bad. I totally understand why you weren't happy to find out she was in Oak Hill and staying at Eternal Rest, no less. Does Danny know about your history with her?"

"I told him yesterday when I gave my statement. A rival I had a beef with was found dead in my office. It doesn't make me look good."

Emily knew there was no point arguing that. If Tessa's

death was determined to be a murder, then Sage might wind up being the top suspect. "All the more reason for us to keep communicating with Tessa," Emily said. "You can't be the only one who had a grudge against her."

"Definitely not. Let's see if we can get something that's actually useful out of her."

Emily closed her eyes again. "Tessa, you have made your feelings about Sage loud and clear. We acknowledge them, and we accept your feelings."

Sage snorted.

"I would like to talk to you about your death," Emily continued. "How did you die? Did someone do this to you?"

Emily had expected to feel her hand twitch again, but instead, a scene began to form in her mind. She was staring at the curtain that led to the consultation space, and Emily realized she was looking through the eyes of someone who was sitting on the sofa. Knowing Tessa must be channeling a memory through her, Emily focused on what she was seeing.

She could hear shallow, labored breathing, and when a loud car rumbled by on the street outside, she felt Tessa's body jerk in fear. A hand reached up and wiped at her brow, coming away wet with sweat. Tessa glanced behind her, toward the door, but it was closed.

Tessa stood and pitched forward, and the memory Emily was seeing in her mind turned black.

Emily's eyes popped open, and she drew in a deep breath, as if she had been underwater. She pressed a splayed hand against her chest. "Sage, I think I saw Tessa's last moments. She was alone, and she was terrified."

"How did she get into my office in the first place?" Sage asked, leaning forward excitedly.

Emily shook her head. "I don't know. Let me ask her."

After several minutes of trying to reach Tessa again,

Emily still hadn't received any kind of response. "Tessa, please," she said, more out of frustration than any real effort to communicate. "If you were murdered, we want to know who did it. We want to help you find your killer."

This time, another scene did appear in Emily's mind, but she knew it wasn't just one single memory. Instead, she saw faces, flashing past at a rapid pace. Each face appeared and was replaced by another so quickly Emily couldn't keep up.

When her mind cleared again, Emily leaned back wearily. "I think Tessa felt like she had a lot of enemies. She just showed me about twenty different people. Unfortunately, it was so quick that I can't tell you who any of them were."

"Tessa was overly dramatic, but she probably isn't exaggerating about how many people disliked her," Sage said thoughtfully. "That's what you get when you're a diva and a fake."

A thick hardback book slid off a shelf high above Sage's head and crashed onto the floor next to her. Sage simply glared up at the shelf and said, "You missed me."

"Sage, I don't recommend taunting the ghost who knows how to throw things," Emily said.

Sage looked at Emily. "And I don't recommend that you keep talking to Tessa. At least, not until later. You're clearly exhausted from your efforts."

"It's definitely time for a lunch break."

As Sage and Emily walked to The Depot, Sage told Emily several times how proud she was of her. "I knew you had it in you, but your psychic medium skills are advancing really quickly," Sage said, peering at Emily through her bright-yellow sunglasses. "I don't know that I've ever seen so much progress in so short a time."

"You've probably never known someone who was as

desperate to talk to a spirit as I am. I'm doing all of this so I can help Scott."

The two women had reached The Depot, which sat on the square in the heart of Oak Hill. The outdoor seating area was only half full, and Emily was looking for an empty table in the shade when Sage waved at someone and began walking toward a table in the far corner. Emily was surprised to see Reed and Trevor seated together.

As Sage slid into one of the empty chairs, Emily said, "I didn't realize it was a party."

Sage nodded. "I thought we could use their input."

Emily was sitting next to Trevor, and she felt her cheeks flush, remembering the way she had spoken to him the day before. Even though she had already apologized, she found herself doing it again. "Hey, I'm really sorry about yesterday. I... I didn't mean to—"

"Emily, you have nothing to be sorry about," Trevor interrupted, his voice gentle. He hesitated and glanced away as he added, "Maybe I should be apologizing to you. You seemed upset that I wasn't at the séance on Saturday night."

Of all the things for Trevor to latch onto from her outburst, Emily hadn't expected it to be that. She averted her own eyes as she said, "I didn't mean to sound like I resent you having a social life."

Trevor actually laughed, but before he could respond further, Sage said in a warning tone, "Here comes Jay. Don't tell him too much."

As the owner of The Depot, Jay prided himself on having both fresh food and fresh gossip. He was making a beeline for their table while wiping his hands on his white apron. "Sage, I was so sorry to hear about what happened at your practice," Jay said as soon as he reached the table. "My condolences on the loss of your colleague. Dessert is on me today, for all of you." With that, he turned and walked away.

Sage stared after Jay, her mouth open in shock.

"That was... unexpected," Reed said.

"Not really," Trevor said. "I went inside when I first got here, and there's a little shrine to Tessa Valentine on the counter. I think Jay was a fan."

"I never thought I'd see Jay too distraught to gossip," Sage said with a note of awe.

Emily could feel her energy recovering as she ate and enjoyed the company of her friends. Even the sunshine that filtered through the leaves above seemed to revive her. Sage answered her phone as they were finishing up, and her conversation was extremely brief and too quiet for Emily to hear. Once Sage hung up, she said, "Danny is on his way over here. He says he has news to share."

"If he doesn't want to tell you over the phone, it's probably not good," Emily warned.

Danny arrived just ten minutes later. As he grabbed a chair from a nearby table and placed it at the head of the one where Emily and her friends sat, she saw him throw a sharp glance at Trevor.

Does he still think there's some kind of rivalry between them for my affections? Emily resisted the urge to roll her eyes.

"Tessa did not die of natural causes," Danny said, glancing at the other tables on the patio to ensure he couldn't be overheard. "She died from lead poisoning."

If Danny had been hoping for a dramatic reaction, then he got it. Everyone gasped, except Reed, who made a noise of disgust. "Do you think she was exposed to lead by accident, or do you think this was intentional?" he asked.

"There was a fair amount in her system," Danny said. "We think someone did this to her. Emily, did she exhibit any symptoms when you were with her? It could have been things like irritability—in regard to both her attitude and her stomach—or personality changes, headaches, even fatigue. All of those things can be signs of lead poisoning."

Emily nodded emphatically. "Yes, she did. The first night, Tessa's assistant told me she had switched to a vegetarian diet to combat some stomach issues. And she had a terrible headache the next morning."

"She was complaining of a headache on Monday afternoon, too, when I took her to the bookshop," Sage noted. She narrowed her eyes at Danny. "Am I a suspect?"

"Technically, yes," Danny admitted. "She died in your office, after all, and we still don't know how she got in there. However, if Tessa was exhibiting symptoms even before arriving in Oak Hill, then it's safe to say you didn't kill her."

Sage made a face of mock relief. "Gosh, thank you. I feel better."

"That means her killer might not even be here in Oak Hill," Reed pointed out. "They may have never been here."

Danny nodded. "Which is why we'll be working with the police in Tessa's hometown of Louisville, too. Speaking of which, I've got to get back to the station. I have a call with them in half an hour."

Danny left after promising to call Emily later with any new developments.

"Why would he call you and not me?" Sage wondered as Danny walked away. "Tessa was found in my shop, after all."

Emily shrugged. "Maybe because her colleagues and her boyfriend are staying with me," she suggested.

"Then we start with them," Trevor said. "Like Reed just said, Tessa's killer might be someone from a different town, but we can start looking at the people who are here in Oak Hill."

"She did have a lot of enemies," Sage said. "With her

diva attitude, I can see how someone close to her might have gotten sick of it and just snapped."

"Actually," Emily said, gazing in the direction of the square, "I'm going to start by questioning someone Tessa didn't know at all."

Sage, Reed, and Trevor turned to see what Emily was looking at. Five people were standing in a line on the grass of the square, and each one of them was holding up a protest sign. From her vantage point, the only one Emily could see read, *Halloween is an abomination.*

"It's only August!" Emily said incredulously. "Halloween is more than two months away!"

"Oh, is that what they're protesting?" Sage sounded completely unsurprised. "Jen said the Chamber of Commerce announced the details yesterday for the Oak Hill Fall Festival. Apparently, they ruffled a few feathers by including plans for a Halloween costume contest."

"That one lady was outside Seeing Beyond yesterday," Trevor said. "Is that who you're going to talk to, Emily?"

"Yeah. She was protesting in front of my house, too. If we're lucky, she saw something helpful while she was shouting about evil psychics. Danny had even considered talking to her, back when we hoped Tessa was just missing."

As soon as Emily paid for her lunch, she rose, said a quick goodbye, and headed in the direction of the protestors. She wasn't surprised when she saw Trevor rushing to catch up with her.

"I can't let you have all the fun," he told her. "Besides, I need to make more friends in this town, and they look like a nice group of folks."

Emily laughed, but she also shot Trevor a warning look. "We're trying to get information out of them, so we're the ones who have to be nice."

The woman who had spearheaded the protest on Emily's lawn put down her sign and crossed her arms defiantly when she saw Emily approaching. Emily actually held up both hands like she was surrendering. "I come in peace," Emily said.

What am I, an alien visitor?

The woman just raised one eyebrow in response.

"We haven't exactly met formally. I'm Emily. Look, I know you didn't like Tessa, but we need to find her killer. Officer Newton said he has a cousin in your group, and I'm sure all of you are eager to help the police with their investigation as much as possible."

The woman's face tightened, and she shifted uncomfortably. "Of course we are."

"You were at Eternal Rest and the office building where Tessa's body was found. If you've been keeping tabs on Tessa, then we're hoping that maybe you saw something suspicious."

"Tessa was the suspicious one. It's no wonder she was killed," the woman said. Emily thought she was going to refuse to say anything more, but then her body relaxed, and she actually reached out to shake Emily's hand. "I'm Bernie Moss. I may not approve of the people you hang out with"—Bernie's eyes flicked in the direction of The Depot, and Emily saw a flash of disdain in them—"but I do appreciate that you're helping the police. Like I said, Tessa was the one acting weird. After I left your B and B, I went on home, but later in the afternoon, when I was out running errands, I saw Tessa walking along the square. I was just coming out of the pharmacy, and I walked into the square to see where she was going."

"To Grainy Day, I assume," Emily said.

"Yeah, but she kept looking behind her, like she thought she was being followed. It wasn't just a glance or two, either. It was almost wild, like she was close to panic."

Bernie's account matched what Trish had said about Tessa's behavior inside the bakery, and Emily wondered if she had gone in there just to put a door between herself and her perceived shadow. That might explain why she had bought baked goods so soon after snacking at the bookstore. She wasn't hungry but hiding out. "Did you see what she did after she left Grainy Day?" Emily asked.

"I followed her almost all the way to the building where she died, but she finally spotted me," Bernie admitted. "That seemed to freak her out even more, and she started to run. I left after that. It was getting a little too bizarre for me."

"You didn't see anyone else following her?" Trevor asked.

Bernie shook her head. "No one that I saw."

Emily thanked Bernie, and as she and Trevor turned away, he leaned toward Emily and said, "If the police are right, and Tessa was being poisoned for a period of time before she finally died, then why would anyone be following her? This isn't a situation where the murderer was tracking down their victim to kill them in the moment."

"Maybe Tessa only thought she was being followed," Emily speculated. "Maybe that threatening note she got made her suspicious of someone here in Oak Hill."

"Or maybe the police are wrong, and this wasn't a long, slow poisoning. How much lead would someone have to be exposed to in order to die in just a day from it?"

Emily wrinkled her nose. "I'm not sure I want to know. It's a good question, though."

Emily was about to step off the sidewalk at the edge of the square so she could rejoin Sage and Reed at The Depot, but Trevor caught her arm. "I have to get back to work," he said, looking at her seriously. "Please be careful, Emily. I don't trust your guests, and if the killer thinks you're hot on their trail…"

"I'll watch what I say," Emily assured him. "And I promise to call you if I need anything."

When Emily slid back into her chair at The Depot, she was happy to sit in thought while Sage and Reed continued some debate that seemed to be about the possibility of zombies. Ordinarily, she would have laughed at the idea, but her friends seemed to be taking it seriously.

"Speaking of zombies," Sage said eventually, waving a hand in front of Emily's face. "Yoo-hoo, are you there?"

Emily blinked, then laughed. "I'm still here." She told them what Bernie had shared about Tessa's apparent paranoia that she was being followed, and she repeated Trevor's theory that Tessa's poisoning hadn't been as long and slow as the police were speculating.

"I think you and Sage have a lot of questions to ask Tessa's ghost," Reed said. "I have to get back to Hilltop—we're just about done leveling the granite barrier around the Carnaby plot, Emily—but call me if you need me."

"We will," Emily promised.

Sage quirked an eyebrow at Emily once it was just the two of them sitting at the table. "Shall we continue our conversation with Tessa?"

"Sure, but let's stop at the store to buy you an umbrella," Emily said, smiling. "Just in case Tessa wants to drop any more books on you."

"I'll be on my best behavior," Sage said, though the glint in her eyes said otherwise. "Let's walk to The

Stomping Grounds first. I mostly have my energy back after all that business with the psychic barrier, but I've gotten used to my after-lunch latte."

Emily and Sage walked the few blocks to The Stomping Grounds, and Emily had to suppress a shudder as she thought about her visit there just two nights before, when she was searching for Tessa. *Was Tessa already dead while I was here looking for her?*

Sage was dumping sugar into her latte, and Emily was blowing on a steaming cup of black coffee when Emily saw someone walking up to them. She was slightly surprised when she realized it was Steven Bates. "Aren't you filming today?" Emily asked, unable to keep a bit of a judgmental tone out of her voice.

"We're taking a little break," Steven answered evenly. "I know it's hard for you to understand my drive to keep filming, even in light of what's happened, but it shouldn't be. One of your guests is dead, but you're still taking reservation requests, aren't you? You haven't kicked the rest of us out of your B and B."

Emily had to admit she hadn't thought of it that way, and Steven continued, "I have a lot of money invested in this show, Emily. I'm doing the best I can to stay afloat. Rylee hasn't made a name for herself yet, and she won't draw as many viewers as Tessa would have, but I've got to try to make this show a success. We all have bills to pay, just like you."

"Get yourself another celebrity psychic," Sage suggested bluntly.

"That could take weeks," Steven said, and Emily surmised he had already considered—and rejected—that option. "I'm not sure I really want another celebrity psychic on my team, anyway. Tessa was so difficult to work with."

"Of course she was." Sage waved a hand. "You should

have known that before you ever started this show with her."

"No, I didn't." When Sage looked at Steven skeptically, he raised one hand as if he were taking an oath. "I swear. I had read all of her books, watched her guest appearances on other TV shows, and of course I spoke to her many times when this was all in the planning stages. She always came off as thoughtful and kind."

"You should have interviewed some of her peers," Sage said.

"I'll do that if there's ever a next time." Steven sighed. "Maybe this is all for the best."

Emily nearly choked on the sip of coffee she had just taken. "Tessa's murder is for the best?"

"No, no. I meant maybe it's for the best that we're no longer working with Tessa," Steven said quickly. "Our production company might be losing a ton of money, but at least we're not going to lose our reputation."

"Why would you lose your reputation?" Emily asked. "Like you just said, Tessa is a celebrity psychic. I would think a TV show starring her would be a huge hit."

Steven's shoulders twitched, and he scratched his head while glancing away. Finally, he said, "I'm just not sure Tessa was as gifted as she claimed to be. Well, she was very gifted, but I don't think her true talent was in mediumship."

Sage laughed sardonically. "I could have told you that!"

"What do you think her true talent was?" Emily asked Steven.

"She was very skilled at making herself look successful. It's easy enough to pull the wool over your fans' eyes when you're writing about yourself in a book, but it's a lot harder to do in front of a camera. I'm fairly certain most of Tessa's alleged interactions with ghosts were completely faked."

15

Sage laughed so long and so loud that several other customers at The Stomping Grounds turned to stare at her. "I was right!" she shouted in triumph.

"Do you think she was just pretending to communicate with ghosts?" Emily asked.

"I think it was a lot more complicated than that," Steven said. "Even on Monday, at the old mill, she said some very specific things about the place. I suspect she did advance research so she could memorize a little history, then repeat it later as if a ghost were describing it to her. Plus, I'm sure you've heard of a cold read?"

"That's a tool a lot of fake psychics use," Sage supplied. "They use cues like facial expressions and body language to create a story that the person they're talking to will believe."

Emily tilted her head. "What do you mean?"

"Let's pretend I'm a fake medium, and you come into my shop for a consultation," Sage said. "I might say, 'I sense someone on the other side who wants to speak with you. Their name starts with an F? Or is that an S?' You would sit up a little straighter and look more eager at that second letter, and so I would lean into it, saying, 'Yes, an S. You were close to someone whose name starts with an S…' You'd probably perk right up and tell me it was your late husband, Scott. From there, I'd just keep making little suggestions in order to gauge what sort of experience you wanted. If you made him sound like a jerk, I'd have his spirit apologize. If he sounded like a nice guy, I'd tell you that he misses you and is always watching over you."

Steven was nodding. "That's exactly what I suspected Tessa of doing."

"When she came into my house," Emily said, "she started talking about all of these sad, miserable male ghosts. She probably figured no one would argue with her. Rylee wouldn't dare to contradict her mentor's pronouncement, and Tessa didn't know that Sage and I have already met all the ghosts at Eternal Rest. Tessa would have figured she could put on a show without worrying about getting caught in the lie."

Emily had already suspected Tessa was just pretending to see all of those ghosts at Eternal Rest, and of all the information Steven had shared, she was most interested in his comment about Tessa doing advance research. Maybe that was why Tessa had asked Sage to drive her to Under the Covers. She wanted to get some more Oak Hill history.

Of course, Emily reasoned, the library would have been a more likely spot to gather local information. Perhaps Tessa had gone to the bookshop to learn more tricks or to look up more generic history. Emily thought of one of the books, about great leaders of the nineteenth century. She wondered if Tessa was planning to have the ghost of Abraham Lincoln make a guest appearance in Oak Hill. Maybe she had been looking for a few historical facts to prove she was communicating with him.

"Speaking of your house," Steven said, interrupting Emily's thoughts, "I haven't given up on getting permission from you to film there. I believe in Rylee's psychic abilities more than I ever did in Tessa's."

"I have to admit, I agree with you there," Emily said.

"I'm still not comfortable with the idea of filming at Eternal Rest, though. The entity that wrecked Rylee's room might not like being the center of attention."

"Maybe that's exactly what it wants," Steven suggested. His phone rang at that moment, and he waved a goodbye to Emily and Sage as he answered it.

Once they were out on the sidewalk and heading in the direction of Seeing Beyond, Emily said, "Do you think Steven killed Tessa to save his show?"

"His show and his reputation," Sage agreed. "If he saw Rylee's potential as an authentic psychic medium, he might have jumped at the opportunity to get Tessa out of the way. Although, it seems pretty ruthless to kill someone and call it a smart business decision."

"We've met people who have killed for less."

Just a few minutes later, Emily was draining her coffee cup as she sat in Sage's consultation area again. "Let's start by asking Tessa about her relationship with Steven," Emily suggested, putting her cup down with a decisive *plunk*.

Before she could even try to establish contact with Tessa to ask her just that, there was a noise above Emily and Sage. Instinctively, both women raised their arms to cover their heads. When nothing fell, Emily stood up and looked. "She just pushed a book out onto the edge of the shelf."

"I guess she has a few things to say about Steven, and she doesn't want to wait," Sage said.

"Tessa, would you like to write through me again?" Emily called as she sat back down. "Tell us if Steven might have been the one who killed you."

Emily's hand jerked forward immediately, and she grabbed the pencil. She felt excited and nervous, and she reminded herself she needed to stay calm and relaxed. Her hand flew over the paper. When her hand finally stopped, Emily put the pencil down and read what Tessa had written through her: *Always watching me. I never felt alone. I didn't like the way he made me feel. I think he was following me.*

"Well," Sage said, sitting back and crossing her arms. "Steven is definitely staying on the suspect list."

"However, we have to consider what Steven himself just told us," Emily said. "He admitted he was keeping a close eye on Tessa to see if she was faking her abilities. She might have noticed his watchfulness."

"Maybe Steven was watching her methods and stalking her with murderous intentions at the same time," Sage countered.

"If he saw something that backed up his belief that Tessa was a fake, he might have decided to get her out of the way," Emily agreed.

This time, the noise overhead was louder than before. Again, Sage and Emily both cringed and ducked their heads. Emily could feel a barrage of books raining down around her, and the corner of one heavy hardback hit her squarely on the back of the neck.

When the books settled, Emily raised her head cautiously. An entire bookshelf had been emptied. "What was that about, Tessa?" Emily called. "We're trying to help you!"

"I've been meaning to sort through my books," Sage said, sounding much calmer than Emily. "I guess Tessa is starting the process for me." Sage leaned forward and said in a whisper, "I think we should avoid using the F-word anymore when we're talking about Tessa."

"The F-word?"

"Fake," Sage mouthed.

"Agreed. Why don't we go sit on the sofa and try again? There aren't any overhead objects there that she can pelt us with."

Sage quickly agreed, but Emily was unable to get a response from Tessa, no matter how many different ways she pleaded. "I think she's giving us the silent treatment," Emily finally said.

"Or she wore herself out with that book stunt. She's still a new ghost, and I'm sure she's still learning how to regulate her energy."

"I'll help you clean up." Emily rose.

Sage waved a hand. "Don't worry about it. Like I said, I've been meaning to sort through my books, anyway. You go home and press your guests for clues."

"Will do."

Emily drove home slowly, mulling over everything they had learned in just a few short hours. It was hard to picture her guests out filming and trying to find random Oak Hill ghosts when one of their own was haunting Seeing Beyond.

"Oh!" Emily blurted. "Of course!" As soon as she was home and parked, she called Sage. "Offer Steven the chance to film at Seeing Beyond! There's no way he would turn that down. He might get some incredible footage, and it keeps Tessa's name tied to the project without threatening Steven's reputation."

Emily could practically hear Sage's smile on the other end of the call. "And it will be great publicity for Seeing Beyond. When my mediumship skills return, I'll be swamped with business."

"Exactly."

The idea of helping Sage with her business made Emily feel slightly better, and for the following hour, she was able to lose herself in taking care of reservation requests. All too soon, though, the first of her guests returned.

Rylee walked into the parlor and sank onto the sofa. She sighed deeply.

Emily spun around in her desk chair and said, "Hi, Rylee. Would you like the parlor to yourself for a while?"

"No, it's okay. I just needed to get away from Vic. Luckily, I was able to talk him into hanging out with the production team for the rest of the day. I appreciate his concern, but he just wouldn't stop fussing over me today. I'm not Tessa. I don't need to be treated like a delicate little princess."

"Why was he fussing over you? Are you feeling okay?"

"I'm just exhausted. There are so many ghosts in this town, Emily! They're everywhere we go, and it's overwhelming. I know that sounds like something Tessa would have said, but it's true."

"I believe you." Emily got up and moved to one of the wingback chairs flanking the sofa. "There's a psychic barrier around Oak Hill, designed to keep evil things out. It weakens over time, and ghosts flocked to Oak Hill before it was strengthened again. We think they feel safe here."

"Of course they do! I'm sure ghosts can feel the pull of this town, just like I do."

Emily leaned forward and narrowed her eyes at Rylee. "What do you mean?"

Rylee brought her hands up to look like she was holding an invisible beach ball. "Oak Hill is special. It's somehow separate from the rest of the world, and it's not just because of that barrier you mentioned. I grew up an hour away from here, and my mom used to bring me with her when she came antique shopping here. Even as a kid, I could feel this town was different. I felt drawn to it."

"Why?"

"There's just something about this place. When I started exploring my abilities as a psychic medium, coming to this area seemed to help. It's almost like my abilities were enhanced when I was here, and I was better able to see and communicate with ghosts. I don't know why Oak Hill is like that; I just know that it is. It's why I told Tessa she should film here."

"Coming to Oak Hill for the TV show was your idea, then," Emily said, slightly surprised.

Rylee nodded, and she seemed to understand Emily's implication. "Not that Tessa would ever admit that to anyone. She looked straight at the camera Monday morning and said she chose Oak Hill because she could feel the psychic pull of the town, and it was like a vortex of paranormal energy that she couldn't resist."

"It must have been tough having a mentor who was so insistent on always being the one in the spotlight," Emily said.

"You have no idea. She would trot me out from time to time, when it served her purposes, but otherwise she was content to let me sit on the sidelines and observe. She used to share a lot of insight with me, and I think she liked the idea of taking someone under her wing, but as my own abilities progressed, she got guarded. She flat-out refused to share her more famous mediumship techniques with me." Rylee sighed. "Now I'll never know how to do them."

"I've heard some of those more famous tricks might have been just that," Emily said carefully.

"Honestly, I think you're right. That could be the real reason she never shared them with me. When Tessa first started mentoring me, I was so honored. I was in awe of her when she was communicating with spirits. As time went on, though, I began to have my doubts about her. Don't get me wrong: I think Tessa was a skilled medium. At some point, though, I think her desire to put on a good show got in the way of giving an accurate reading. Maybe her death was for the best. No one ever has to know whether or not she was faking some things, and I don't have to hide in her shadow anymore."

Emily had an odd feeling of déjà vu. Steven had said nearly the exact same thing about Tessa's death possibly being for the best. For Rylee and Steven, that meant the best for themselves, and certainly not for Tessa.

"That's a bold thing to say, considering the police are still looking for Tessa's killer," Emily said. Rylee was suddenly on her suspect list, vying for the top spot with Steven.

"I didn't kill her," Rylee said defensively. "For all of her faults, I loved Tessa like a big sister. Now, I just feel kind of lost. Steven is making me the star of his TV show, but does it even matter? He says we won't get the same viewership without Tessa's name attached to it."

"I was actually thinking about that," Emily said. "Tessa's ghost is haunting Seeing Beyond, so why not film there? Tessa can still be a part of the TV show, in a way, and I bet viewers would flock to a show featuring her ghost."

Rylee stared at Emily, her mouth moving but no words coming out. After a few attempts to say something, she finally stammered, "Tessa… Tessa's ghost?"

"Yes. Sage and I were communicating with her earlier." Emily eyed Rylee carefully. She had been thinking that filming at Seeing Beyond would be a way to get some more answers from Tessa, and she hadn't stopped to think how Rylee would take the news that her former mentor was haunting the scene of her death. Emily wasn't sure if she had expected surprise or pleasure, but it certainly hadn't been this stunned shock.

"But... How... Are you sure?" Rylee's hands were twisting together nervously in her lap.

"Oh, yeah. We had two séances with her today. Both times, she made it clear that she doesn't like anyone suggesting she was a fraud. It's definitely Tessa I was communicating with."

"Did she say anything about me?" Rylee's voice was so quiet Emily had to lean forward even farther to hear her.

"No. Why, is there something you don't want Tessa to tell us?" Emily felt a stab of worry.

Rylee's face crumpled, and she brought her hands up to her face as she started to cry. "We had a fight. Sunday night. And now she's dead!"

"What did you fight about?"

It was a few moments before Rylee could control her crying enough to answer in a quavering voice, "I confronted her about claiming there were all those ghosts in the parlor with us. I told her I hadn't sensed them, and that I didn't think she really had, either."

Emily couldn't begin to imagine how much that accusation must have hurt Tessa's pride. "You seemed to have made up by breakfast on Monday morning," Emily noted.

"Not really. She had that headache, remember? She never said a word to me until we got to the old mill. I think those protesters put her in a good mood, so she finally forgot all about our fight. Still, I hate that one of the last things I ever said to her was accusing her of faking her abilities. And if the police find out, they're going to think I killed her!"

As Rylee had been talking, Emily had felt herself relaxing. Rylee was upset, but that one fight certainly didn't make Rylee guilty of murder. She was still a suspect in Emily's eyes, though. "The police think Tessa's poisoning had been going on for a while," Emily said gently. "They're going to be looking further back than the night before her disappearance."

Rylee wiped at her eyes and blew out her breath. "That makes me feel better. And I would like to talk to Tessa's spirit, whether or not it's being filmed. I'd like to apologize to her."

"I'm sure we can make that happen."

The front door banged open, and a few seconds later, Vic stalked into the parlor. He looked scared and angry, and he was breathing heavily. Rylee turned around to get a better look at him. "Vic, are you okay? What happened?"

"Someone nearly ran me off the road just now. I was on my way here, and a car coming toward me veered all the way over the yellow line. If I hadn't swerved onto the shoulder, they would have run right into me! I missed slamming into a tree by about a foot." Vic sat down next to Rylee, who put an arm around his shoulders and looked at him anxiously.

Vic reached up and squeezed Rylee's hand. "I'm okay," he said. "Just really shaken up."

"Do you think someone did it on purpose?" Rylee pressed.

"Probably just a drunk driver," Vic said, leaning his head on Rylee's shoulder. "Right?"

"Right." Rylee didn't sound convinced at all.

Emily had noticed the way Rylee was looking at Vic, and how closely they were sitting together. For the first time, she began to wonder if there was more to their relationship than just an assistant and his client's protégé.

She was also wondering if Vic's experience wasn't just a random encounter with a bad driver. Someone had killed

Tessa for a reason, and it was possible that reason had something to do with Vic, too.

"What did the car look like?" Emily asked.

Vic raised his head and stared out the parlor windows, but his unfocused gaze told Emily he was replaying the incident in his mind. "Some kind of SUV that was black, or maybe dark blue," he finally said. "It all happened so quickly, and by the time I got back onto the road, the car had disappeared around a turn. I thought about turning around to follow them, but then what? Yell at them at a stop sign?"

"You made the right decision to come back here," Rylee said. "It was the safest choice. Emily, are there restaurants in town that will deliver out here? I think we should stay in tonight."

"Of course," Emily assured her. Rylee, it seemed, was also thinking this hadn't been a random incident and that perhaps Vic had been meant to crash his car.

Emily gave Vic and Rylee a list of Oak Hill restaurants that would deliver, then Rylee led the way toward the stairs. As she and Vic walked out of the parlor, Rylee glanced over her shoulder. "I don't like this," she said quietly to Vic.

As soon as she was the only one left in the parlor, Emily called Danny. She let him know what Vic had told her, ending with, "It could just be a coincidence, of course, but it seems like strange timing that Tessa's assistant would have a close call two days after Tessa's own murder."

"Agreed," Danny said. He was quiet for a few moments, and Emily expected he was scribbling down the details she had just shared. Eventually, he continued, "Have you eaten dinner yet? I can bring something over to the house, if you want."

"Oh, thanks, but I need to get a few things done around here," Emily said, feeling suddenly awkward. How many times was she going to have to turn Danny down before he finally stopped asking?

"Okay," Danny answered. "I'll talk to you tomorrow." He sounded mildly annoyed.

"Danny," Emily began, trying to think of something to say that would be kind but not misleading. It was too late, though. Danny had already hung up.

Emily put her phone down with a frustrated grunt. "Men."

When Trish arrived shortly after with her delivery of baked goods, Emily welcomed the distraction. She knew gossip about Tessa's murder would be inevitable, but what she hadn't expected was for Trish to announce, "Guess who's been getting drunk at Sutter's since two o'clock this afternoon? That producer guy!"

"Steven? Oh, no. Sage and I ran into him at The Stomping Grounds, and he told us he was just on a break from filming."

Trish waggled her eyebrows. "Apparently, he extended his break. I guess he decided he wanted beer more than coffee."

Emily reached out and grabbed two of the bags from Trish's hands. "I guess I'd be having a drink, too, if the star of my TV show were dead. I wonder if I should tell Rylee and Vic so they can go pick him up."

"Oh, I wouldn't worry about it," Trish said, waving a hand. "Surely he's back in his hotel room by now, probably passed out. Sutter would have called him a taxi, of course."

"You're probably right. One of my guests hasn't come back, either. Tessa's boyfriend, Brian. Maybe he's with Steven. He's not losing money over Tessa's death like Steven is, but I'm sure he's got just as much reason to drink."

"Poor guy." Trish shared some more gossip, this time

about a few local farmers who were feuding, then wished Emily a good night.

As the evening wore on, Emily realized she was listening for the front door to open. She made dinner, ate, and cleaned up, and still, Brian hadn't returned. If he was with Steven, then the two of them had been at Sutter's for hours.

When the doorbell rang, Emily answered it eagerly, but it was just a food delivery for Rylee and Vic. As she passed the bag to Vic, who had come downstairs while Emily was answering the door, she asked him if he knew where Brian might be.

"He told me earlier he was going to head into town for the evening," Vic said, sounding completely unconcerned. "I'll text him."

Emily returned to the parlor and was working on her budgeting when she caught a slight movement out of the corner of her eye. Her hands froze over the laptop keyboard, and she held her breath as she watched the pen moving by itself over the blank piece of paper sitting next to her laptop.

Finally, Kelly was writing a message right in front of Emily.

Emily was so excited, and so gratified, that Kelly finally felt comfortable enough to write a message without making Emily turn her back first that she was barely even paying attention to what the words said. It was only after the pen fell over that she finally read Kelly's note.

Scary ghost is busy. Scott is here now, while it's safe.

"Kelly, thank you, thank you, thank you!" Emily clasped her hands together and rested her chin on them. She shut her eyes and tried to reach out with her mind, imagining her consciousness spreading through the parlor. "Scott, are you here?" Emily realized her voice was shaking in anticipation.

Emily felt a shiver run up her spine, and she had the distinct feeling someone was standing behind her. "Scott?" she asked again.

There was no answer she could actually hear, but the word *here* formed in her mind.

"Where have you been?"

Again, words popped into Emily's mind, even though no voice was actually speaking them. *In the cemetery. Hiding from her.*

"Who is she, anyway? Why is she after you?"

This time, Emily did hear an actual voice. It had been nearly three years since she had heard it, but she recognized it immediately.

"I'll tell you everything, but first, let me see your beautiful blue eyes. Turn around, Emily."

Emily opened her eyes and turned slowly in her chair, her heart pounding in her chest.

Scott was standing there, a smile on his face and a faint glow around his ghostly form.

Thoughts were flooding through Emily's mind. All the things she wanted to say to Scott bubbled to the surface: how much she missed him, how strange it was to see this slightly transparent version of her husband, and, more than anything, how relieved she felt that he was finally there.

"Welcome home," Emily whispered. Scott's ghost wavered, and for a brief moment, she thought his form was weakening, until she realized it was simply tears obscuring her vision. Emily wiped her eyes, hoping Scott wouldn't disappear when she blinked.

Emily stood and took a step toward Scott. He was only a foot away from her, and Emily could feel the cold radiating off him.

"I wish I could give you a kiss," Scott said wistfully.

"Me, too. It's so good to see you, Scott."

"How long has it been, Emily? Time is different on this plane. When did I die?"

"It will be three years ago next month. It's August now."

"You've been on your own for three years already? I'm so sorry."

Emily shook her head. "You have nothing to be sorry about. The car crash wasn't your fault."

"I have a lot to be sorry about." Scott smiled sadly. "I'm sorry I wasn't strong enough to fight her off. I'm sorry I caused you pain. I'm sorry I left you all alone."

"I always thought there was something strange about the crash, and I never gave up hope that your ghost was still around so we could find answers together."

"It took me a long time to get back to Oak Hill, and then that barrier was just too strong for me to get through. I saw you so many times when you were walking through the cemetery. You were so close, but I had no way to let you know I was there."

"And then we finally got you through, only for you to have to hide out from the entity."

Scott glanced in the direction of Hilltop Cemetery. "I hid in the cemetery, and it was surprisingly beneficial. As you can see, I'm much stronger now. I met a ghost who says he's been haunting the Eisen mausoleum for a while, and he taught me a lot about how to harness energy."

Emily actually chuckled. "Is he the one who's been banging on things over there?"

"Yeah. He was a drummer in a rock band, back in the 1960s. He says the acoustics in the mausoleums are fantastic." Scott grinned, the skin around his green eyes crinkling in delight. "He came through the barrier when it was weak so he would be protected from the evil things out there."

"Evil things like the entity. Who is she?" Emily asked again.

Scott's grin disappeared. "She's just a child."

"What? After everything I've experienced with that entity, I can't believe it's just the ghost of a little girl."

"It's not anymore, but that's what she was when I first met her. I was just a child myself then. After I died, she made me remember things that I'd forgotten. Her ghost found its way to our house, and she was my friend. We played together. Then, one day, I just started ignoring her."

"That was probably the day your mom gave you your necklace. It was an amulet to block your psychic abilities."

"Exactly. I wasn't ignoring her at all. I simply couldn't see or sense her anymore, but she didn't know that. Of course, I didn't know what the necklace did until right before I died, when my mom finally told me I had exhibited psychic abilities when I was little."

"She did it to keep you safe," Emily said. "Darlene said you were beginning to see scary things, and she wanted to shield you from them."

"And it worked. Eventually, I guess I just forgot all about the little girl. She didn't forget about me, though. She continued to haunt our home for years, thinking I was ignoring her and being mean to her. She got more and more angry with me."

"What was her name?"

"Lily. She was seven when she died of scarlet fever. She must have been a ghost for nearly a century before I came along."

"She had finally found a friend, who suddenly just started acting like she wasn't there at all," Emily supplied. She was surprised to feel a stab of sympathy for the entity. "She must have been so lonely."

"By the time I went to visit my mom three years ago, Lily's anger had replaced anything that was once good about her. It had transformed her from a little girl into something that wasn't really a ghost anymore. It was more like a concentration of negative psychic energy. She can barely communicate in whole sentences. Instead, she sort of transmits feelings to me. Hate, resentment, even sadness. I had dreamed about her during that visit to my mom, but when I left to come home, I hadn't even stopped to consider that she might follow me."

"You told me during our last phone call that you wanted to find ways to protect our house spiritually."

Scott gazed around the parlor. "Yes. Mom had told me about the psychic barrier around Oak Hill, but she warned that its strength faded over time and had to be renewed every ten years. I wanted to make sure Eternal Rest was as safe as it could be for us. If Lily could become so dark and threatening, I knew there were other terrible things out there, too. Of course, I never made it home. She followed me and made me crash."

"Did she kill you to get revenge?"

"No. She didn't do it for revenge, Emily. She did it because she wanted her friend back."

Emily felt goose bumps break out on her arms. "She killed you so she could keep you all to herself," she said, horrified. "She wanted you to be a ghost, just like her."

"Yes."

Emily sidestepped Scott and walked to the sofa, where she sank down and buried her face in her hands. When the right side of her body began to grow cold, she knew Scott was sitting next to her. "That poor child," Emily said. "What she did to you is awful, but think of how tormented she must have been that it twisted her into such an evil thing to begin with. She was just a scared, lonely child, and her anger and loneliness turned her into a monster."

"You said it hasn't even been three years since I died, and yet, in such a relatively short period of time, I've had moments where I felt overwhelming despair. There was nothing to free me from her, not even death. I've tried to explain to her what happened, but she either won't listen to me, or her transformation has made her incapable of understanding. She followed me everywhere, sucking my energy away to keep me bound to this plane and to her. Not being able to escape Lily made me feel like a prisoner."

"You *were* her prisoner."

"You're right. Still, I began to understand that if I

could feel so desperate and alone in such a short span of time, it must have been even worse for her to be alone for so many years. If I had been in her situation, who's to say I wouldn't have become a monster, too?"

"You feel sorry for her." Emily wasn't even asking a question. She recognized the pity in his voice.

"She needs peace as much as I do."

Emily finally lifted her head and looked at Scott. It was thrilling to look into his eyes again, and to see him sitting just inches away from her on the sofa. At the same time, though, it was strange. He was there, but she couldn't reach out and take his hand. Emily realized it wasn't just strange; it was also sad. It was a relief to finally be talking to Scott, but his ghost only reminded her of what she'd lost.

"Emily?" Scott prompted. He leaned toward her, one hand reaching for hers. Emily could feel the icy cold emanating from his fingers.

Emily sniffed and glanced away, willing herself not to cry. "Sorry. It's just that I've really missed you, and seeing you again reminds me just how much." She cleared her throat and gave her head a shake to clear out those thoughts. She returned her gaze to Scott and asked, "How do we help Lily?"

"I'm not even sure we can, but we need to try. She needs to understand that crossing over is the best chance she has at not being lonely anymore. She can find her family, and she can have peace."

"Before she can do that, though, she needs to let you go."

Scott nodded. "I thought maybe Sage could have a talk with her."

"Sage lost her abilities when we brought you through the barrier," Emily admitted. "However, I've been learning to communicate with ghosts myself. I don't like the idea of talking to Lily again—like I said, she threatened me and Sage a couple of times—but I'll give it a shot. If we help her, then we'll be better able to help you."

"Thank you, Emily. Hopefully the ghosts here can help, too. Kelly is definitely eager to be a part of the team."

Emily smiled. "Kelly is great. Do you know how she wound up here?"

"I do. I also know that you're the one who figured out who had killed her. In fact, I understand—" Scott cut off abruptly and whipped his head toward the parlor door. "I have to go," he said in a rush. He gave Emily one last look and disappeared.

"Scott?" Emily cried, reaching toward the spot where her husband's ghost had just been. Her voice was still echoing through the room when she heard slow footsteps coming down the stairs.

18

Emily jumped up and faced the doorway, ready for whatever might come through it. Her fear was that Lily had found Scott and was coming for him.

"She's going to have to deal with me instead," Emily grumbled to herself. She felt slightly ridiculous when she realized her hands were curled into fists, as if she were preparing to punch a ghost in the face.

There were a few quiet steps in the hallway, and then Rylee appeared in the doorway.

Emily's fear that it was Lily instantly turned into fear that something bad had happened to Rylee. Her face was even paler than usual, and she looked a little unsteady on her feet. Emily rushed forward and took Rylee by one elbow, guiding her gently to the sofa.

"I'm okay," Rylee said softly, her voice quavering.

"What happened?" Before she could give Rylee a chance to respond, Emily continued, "It was that ghost, wasn't it? The girl who trashed your room."

Rylee nodded slowly.

"Did she hurt you?" Emily sat down next to Rylee and peered closely at her, looking for any signs that Lily had lashed out violently.

"No. I don't think she wants to hurt me. I think she just wants someone to talk to."

"That makes sense. I was actually talking to Scott before you came downstairs, and after everything he told me about her, I realize she's scared and lonely. She knows you can sense her, and so she's trying to make a friend, I think."

"A friend? But you said before she's a dark entity."

"She is, but she wasn't always like that. Come on, let's go sit in the kitchen, and I'll explain everything. What's going to make you feel better: a cup of tea or a glass of wine?"

"Tea, please." Rylee followed Emily to the kitchen and sank down into one of the chairs at the table while Emily put the kettle on. As she waited for the water to boil, Emily told Rylee everything Scott had relayed to her. By the time she was finished, Rylee had perked up significantly and was nodding in agreement. "There's still some part of the child left. She's not all evil."

"I hope that's the case. Like I said, Rylee, she was probably trying to make friends with you. I think she trashed your room to get attention. You said yourself that it felt like the ghost was being petulant. A child stomping her feet in frustration because she wants somebody to pay attention to her."

Emily put a cup of chamomile tea down in front of Rylee, who pulled it toward herself gratefully and said, "When we were communicating just now, she showed me images, memories of hers that flashed through my mind. It was like I was seeing things through her eyes. Reading a book under a big tree, running through a field with a couple of other kids, petting a cat. Then I was in a big canopy bed, with a woman in a white apron bending over me and looking really sad. I think it was shortly before she died."

"It's encouraging that she remembers those things. If we can remind her of all the loved ones waiting for her on the other side, we'll have a better chance of getting her to cross over." Emily sat down across from Rylee, her own cup of tea cradled in her hands. "And I really mean the 'we' part. If you're willing, I would love to have your help with this, even if it means I have to let Steven film here."

Rylee shook her head decisively. "I will be happy to help, but this is about your late husband as much as it is about this girl Lily. That seems a little too personal for a TV show. I think we shouldn't even mention it to Steven."

"Thanks."

Emily went to bed feeling utterly exhausted but encouraged that she was making progress in helping Scott. She realized he had only come out of hiding in the first place because Lily had been busy communicating with Rylee. It had been the perfect opportunity for Scott to safely speak to Emily. It was also encouraging that Rylee seemed able to break through Lily's anger and resentment in a way Scott couldn't. That gave Emily hope that the lonely little girl Lily had once been was still there, not gone but simply hiding under the turbulent surface.

On Thursday morning, it was impossible for Emily to sit in one place for more than five minutes. She tried to sit at the kitchen table for her first cup of coffee, but soon she was up, finding little tasks to do around the kitchen. It was the same in the parlor. Instead of being able to sit at her desk and focus on work, she got up to adjust the curtains, fluff the sofa cushions, or any other little task that let her get out some of the anxious energy coursing through her. When Clint called to remind Emily he would be coming in late because he had to go get his physical in order to play high school football, she paced back and forth during the entire conversation.

The second the clock read nine, Emily called Sage, hoping she wasn't waking her up.

"Good morning, Em!" Sage answered happily.

"It is a good morning," Emily agreed. She told Sage about her conversation with Scott, and Emily could sense just how sincerely Sage meant it when she told Emily she was happy for her.

"It's also a good morning because I think my abilities are beginning to come back," Sage said. "I woke up early this morning—well, early for me—and I just had this overwhelming sense that I needed to get to Seeing Beyond. Nothing really happened when I got there, but I could sense Tessa. It was a watchful feeling, like someone was standing right behind me."

"Sage, that's great! I knew you'd begin to recover your mediumship skills."

"I still have a long way to go, but it's a step in the right direction. Oh, by the way, I picked up a newspaper on the way over here. Have you seen it?"

"I grabbed it off the front porch, but I haven't read it yet. Is there something in there about Tessa's murder?"

"Boy, is there! That protestor you talked to wrote a letter to the editor. If she was trying to make herself a suspect in the case, then she has accomplished her goal. Go read it. I'm going to keep trying to sense Tessa."

Emily hung up and immediately grabbed the newspaper off her desk. She flipped to the page that had letters to the editor and began to read the one from Bernie Moss as she began to pace again. Bernie wrote that Tessa's death had been just, and that those who supported her career would meet a bad end, too, in punishment for associating with a psychic. Emily read the sentence several times, shocked that Bernie would write something that made herself look so suspicious. Emily thought of Vic's report that someone had nearly run him off the road, and she returned to the idea that it hadn't been a random incident. Now that Tessa was dead, were the members of her team next? And was Bernie the one behind it?

Worried that Rylee and Vic were both in danger, as well as Steven and the rest of the production team, Emily continued reading Bernie's letter. She went on to talk about the bad influence psychics had on their communities, and she recounted how she had been visiting friends in Savannah earlier in the year, during the same weekend as a psychic fair there. *That's where I first saw Tessa Valentine with my own eyes,* Bernie continued, *though I already knew plenty about her. When I confronted her, she called me names I refuse to repeat and had the two men in her entourage push me out of her way.*

Emily stopped pacing and dropped the newspaper onto her desk. The two men Bernie referenced, Emily knew, must be Vic and Brian. That meant Bernie knew what they looked like, and it would have been easy for her to learn which car was Vic's so she could run him off the road.

The letter also meant Bernie's history with Tessa dated back months. She would have had plenty of time to poison her slowly.

Emily called Danny immediately and told him her speculation. "It would have been easy for Bernie to follow Tessa from place to place since she posted her upcoming appearances on her social media," Emily told him. "Bernie could have shown up under the guise of a protestor, while secretly finding a way to poison Tessa."

Danny was quiet for a moment, then he said, "You're right. Well done, Emily. I'll talk to Bernie today and find out if she's been traveling lately."

"Thanks, Danny. Okay, I'll catch up with you later."

"Wait, Emily," Danny said hurriedly. "Before you go, I want to apologize. Last night, when I suggested bringing dinner over to your house, I didn't mean for it to seem so suggestive. I could tell by the way you answered me that you thought I was being too forward. I just thought you might enjoy some company and not having to cook. You've gone through a lot recently. As much as I want to ask you out, I know that's not where you are right now."

Emily thought of Scott sitting next to her on the sofa just the night before. No, she was definitely not in a place to even consider dating someone. "Thanks, Danny. I appreciate you clarifying. The next time you offer, I'll say yes. I can always use the company of a friend."

After her call with Danny ended, Emily was finally able to sit down and relax. She was making progress in helping Scott, Sage was beginning to recover her abilities, and Danny had remembered that she wasn't looking for anything romantic. And as worried as she was about the safety of her guests, at least they were safe at the moment. She could hear the clink of silverware against plates coming from the dining room.

With her mind somewhat settled, Emily tackled some work on her laptop before throwing a load of laundry into the washing machine. She had been great about keeping up with guest sheets and towels, but lately, her own dirty clothes pile had been turning into a mountain.

Emily had just sat down again at her desk when her phone rang. She was surprised to see Trish's name on the caller ID, and she answered quickly, wondering if it was something to do with Clint and his doctor's appointment. "Hey, Trish."

"Emily, have you heard?" Trish sounded upset, and she spoke in a rush.

"Heard what? Hang on, I'm getting another call." Emily held her phone away from her ear and saw that it was Danny trying to call her. Danny wouldn't be calling Emily so soon if he didn't have big news to share. Instantly, she knew that whatever Trish was calling about must be bad.

Emily steeled herself and said, "Tell me, Trish."

"That producer guy was found dead this morning!"

19

"Steven is… dead?" Emily wondered if she had simply misheard Trish.

"Yeah. A couple of customers just came in and told me. His body was found along the road a short way from Sutter's about an hour ago. It looks like he tried to walk from the bar back to his hotel, but he never made it."

"How awful." Emily sat in stunned silence until the memory of Vic's story the night before rose in her mind. "Was he hit by a car?"

"I don't know," Trish admitted. "The cops were already cordoning off the area when my customers drove past. Apparently, Steven wasn't right by the roadside. Otherwise, he would have been found sooner."

"Thanks for letting me know, Trish."

"Yeah. I figured you should be one of the first to know since your guests are—er, were—working with him."

Emily could feel two emotions vying in her for dominance: sadness that Steven was dead and a sickening dread that she was going to have to tell her guests.

The walk into the dining room seemed to happen in slow motion. When Emily reached the doorway, she stopped and stared at the scene in front of her. Rylee was clutching Vic's hands with both of hers, and the two of them were staring at each other with a look of panic.

"You already know," Emily blurted.

Vic turned slowly to face Emily, twisting around awkwardly in his chair so he didn't have to let go of Rylee's hands. "Detective Hernandez just called us. First Tessa, now Steven. Someone is after our team."

"And I don't think the car that ran Vic off the road last night was just a drunk driver," Rylee added. "I think Vic was supposed to die, too."

Emily made a calming gesture with her hands, and even though she was thinking exactly the same thing, she said, "We don't know that for sure, but I do know Danny is going to consider every possibility. In the meantime, I am so sorry for your loss."

In response, Rylee started crying.

Vic began saying something quietly to Rylee, and Emily suddenly felt like she was intruding on a private moment between two grieving people. She began to turn, then stopped and looked back at Rylee and Vic. "Where's Brian?" she asked.

Vic shrugged. "Sleeping it off, I guess."

"When did he get back last night?" *And how,* Emily asked herself, *did I not hear him? I'm a light sleeper, so the noise of him walking up the stairs should have woken me up.*

Rylee dabbed at her eyes with a napkin. "I never heard him come in."

"Me, neither." Vic looked at Emily worriedly. "Do you think…?"

"That something bad happened to Brian, too?" Rylee finished.

Vic was still looking at Emily, and she saw the subtle way his mouth turned down at Rylee's suggestion. "That's not what I was going to say," he said quietly. "If Brian never came back last night, then maybe he killed Steven."

Rylee shook her head. "No. No way. Steven was killed

by the same person who killed Tessa. I'm sure of it. Brian would never have killed her. He was so in love with her!"

"We don't know yet if Steven's death was a murder," Emily reminded Rylee.

"Yes, we do," Vic said. "Detective Hernandez said Steven was strangled."

Emily took three steps forward and dropped into the nearest chair. She braced her elbows on the dining room table and rested her head in her hands. "I didn't know," she said. She was mentally kicking herself for assuming Brian had come back to Eternal Rest at some point, and that he had been upstairs, safe and asleep, during the night. At the moment, it didn't matter whether Rylee's theory that Brian was in danger or Vic's fear that Brian was a killer was correct. All that mattered was that they find Brian as quickly as possible.

Rylee produced her cell phone, and soon, she was holding it up to her ear. Her index finger tapped against the phone nervously. "He's not answering," she said after a few moments, her voice quavering.

"We're going to the police station," Emily said, rising. "Danny needs to know Brian is missing, and I don't know that I want the three of us here by ourselves when there might be a killer coming after everyone involved in the TV show."

"What are we going to do, hang out at the police station all day?" Vic asked, wrinkling his nose.

"If that's what it takes to keep you two safe, yes. Once we've filled Danny in, I'm going to Seeing Beyond to try communicating with Tessa's ghost again. I want to know who had a grudge against both her and Steven."

"Take me with you," Rylee said. "If you want, we can ask a police officer to go with us for protection, but please, let me talk to Tessa, too."

Emily considered briefly, then nodded. "Okay. Vic, you can come, too, if you like."

"Please do," Rylee said, turning pleading eyes to him. "I could use the moral support, and I'll be worried about you if you're not with me."

Vic nodded solemnly. "It sounds better than sitting at the police station like a prisoner." He nodded toward Emily. "We'll run upstairs and finish getting ready. Give us twenty minutes."

Vic and Rylee didn't actually take twenty minutes, but the entire time they were upstairs, Emily paced back and forth in the parlor again. While she trod across the wooden floor, she issued instructions to Kelly. "If Scott comes around, let him know we have a plan, and that I'll be back later. And please keep an eye on the house while we're gone. I want to know if anyone unexpected shows up, since they might be a suspect."

Emily pivoted on her heel when she reached the parlor doorway to make another lap, and she was just in time to see the pen lift, seemingly on its own. Kelly's message was brief and enthusiastic. *You got it* was followed by two exclamation points and a happy face.

Rylee walked into the parlor as Emily was reading Kelly's message. "Oh, did one of your ghosts write that?" Rylee peered at the paper. "I love that you have ghosts on your staff."

Emily smiled. "I hadn't thought about it like that."

"I'm sorry I won't be able to communicate with Lily just yet," Rylee said. "Maybe when we get back later?"

"That would be great, thank you." Emily put a gentle hand on Rylee's shoulder. "Still, you've just lost another friend. Take the time you need to grieve. If I have to wait to help Scott, then I'll wait."

Vic called from the hallway, "Are you two ready? I'll drive."

Emily wasn't entirely sure she wanted to ride with Vic, just in case someone was waiting to try to run him off the road again, but she agreed. She retrieved her purse from her bedroom and slid past Vic and Rylee to open the front door.

The door creaked open, and Emily was already beginning to step over the threshold when she realized something was lying on her welcome mat.

No, not something. Someone.

It was Brian, curled up in a ball on the doorstep, his arms raised to cover his face.

Rylee screamed at the same time Vic yelled, "He's dead!"

Emily bent at the waist and stared at Brian. His shoulders were moving faintly, in time with soft breathing. "He's just asleep." She straightened up and held her nose. "And from the smell of it, I think he drank a lot last night."

Vic wedged himself in the doorway next to Emily and poked at Brian's back with a toe. "Brian, wake up!" he said loudly. "Hey!"

"Mmm… Hmm?" Slowly, Brian moved his arms away from his face, and he squinted up at Emily. "Heyyy…"

"Get up, Brian. You passed out on the porch." Vic reached down and grabbed Brian by the arm, hauling him up.

Brian was unsteady on his feet, and he grabbed the doorframe to balance himself. "I rang the doorbell, but no one answered. I had to sleep out here."

"I don't know what you pressed," Rylee said, "but it wasn't the doorbell."

"Besides, you could have just knocked," Vic added.

"Or walked right in. The door was unlocked," Emily said. Unlike Rylee and Vic, who seemed annoyed and maybe even a little embarrassed for Brian, Emily was trying not to laugh. Brian was in rough shape, but he was safe. And, if he had spent the night on the front porch, that meant Emily could check her security camera to see what time Brian had finally gotten back to Eternal Rest. It might help them determine whether or not he was a suspect in Steven's murder.

"Is there coffee?" Brian stumbled forward, and Emily and Vic both had to move hastily out of the way.

Rylee clicked her tongue impatiently. "I'll pour it for you, and then you're going to brush your teeth and take a shower. You reek."

As Rylee and Vic tended to Brian, Emily went to her desk, opened her laptop, and pulled up her security camera footage from the night before. The front porch camera had captured the moment Brian had gotten back to Eternal Rest. He had, in fact, extended a finger toward the doorbell, but Emily guessed he must have missed it entirely. The time stamp was just before midnight. That meant that if Brian had murdered Steven, then he had done it earlier in the evening.

Emily hoped the police would be able to narrow down the time of Steven's death. At the moment, there was no way to know if Brian was guilty of anything more than having breath that made Emily want to hold her nose.

That meant there was also no way to know if he was responsible for both Tessa's and Steven's deaths. As a precaution, Emily texted Clint, telling him to head home after his physical. *Don't worry,* she typed. *Everything is okay. I'll explain later.* The last thing Emily wanted was for Clint to work his shift, alone, with a possible murderer in the house. Trish would never forgive her if that happened. For that matter, Kelly might not, either.

Rylee was still eager to go to Seeing Beyond, and even Vic seemed more enthusiastic about the idea. As Vic drove them toward Oak Hill, Rylee told Emily that Brian said he had gone to Sutter's to meet Steven.

"I haven't told him about Steven," Rylee said. "I don't know if I was afraid to say anything in case he's responsible for it, or if I just didn't have the heart to give him such bad news."

"Maybe it was a little bit of both," Emily said. "Death can really stir up some conflicting feelings."

Even though Brian was safe and sound, Emily still directed Vic to the police station. She walked into Danny's office with Vic and Rylee trailing after her, and she could hear officers in the hallway commenting to each other in surprise. Emily wondered vaguely how long it would take for news of their visit to reach Trish at Grainy Day.

Even Danny looked surprised to see Emily. He was on the phone when she walked in, and he hastily ended the call and stood up with a worried expression.

"We're okay," Emily began, "but we might have a lead for you." She told Danny that Brian had been with Steven at Sutter's, and that he hadn't gotten back to Eternal Rest until shortly before midnight.

"That's good to know," Danny said. "From the description Sutter gave us, we assumed it was Brian who was with Steven. Brian left an hour before Steven, around eight."

"He could have hidden somewhere and waited for Steven to leave, then followed him," Emily suggested.

"Steven left around nine. Even if Brian hung out for an hour to waylay him, then what did Brian do for the three hours between killing Steven and arriving at Eternal Rest? Did he go somewhere else? Did he walk all the way back to Eternal Rest? I'm going to ask him to come here so we can have a talk. Until then, I don't want any of you under the same roof as Brian until we know whether it's safe for you."

"That's why we're here," Vic said, sounding bored. "Emily wanted to keep an eye on us."

Danny looked at Vic sharply. "She's trying to keep you alive. You should be thanking her."

"We're heading to Seeing Beyond now," Emily said, jumping in before Vic could retort. "We'll go get lunch after we talk to Tessa's ghost, and then I'll check in with you to find out if we can safely head back home." Emily paused, then added, "Actually, you're welcome to join us for lunch."

Danny's face relaxed, and he gave Emily a wide smile. "I'll be scarfing down a sandwich here at my desk, but I appreciate the offer."

As Emily led the way back down the hallway toward the front door of the police station, she heard Rylee ask Vic in a quiet but curious voice, "Is Emily dating the detective?"

Emily kept walking, pretending she hadn't overheard.

When the three of them reached the door of Seeing Beyond, Emily paused with her hand on the doorknob. She could hear Sage's voice, speaking in the low, sonorous tone she used when she was communicating with ghosts. Emily put a finger to her lips to let Rylee and Vic know to remain quiet, then she silently pressed her ear against the door. Sage began speaking again, and even though Emily couldn't discern what she was saying, she could hear a note of excitement.

Sage spoke a few more times, always with a long lull between whatever she was saying, and then Emily distinctly heard the sound of footsteps coming toward the door. She straightened up just as Sage flung the door open.

Emily felt her cheeks flush, and she laughed at herself for feeling like she had been caught doing something wrong. "I wasn't trying to eavesdrop," she told Sage, "but I didn't want to interrupt whatever you were doing in there."

Sage grinned. "I," she said proudly, "was having a little chat with Tessa Valentine."

Emily threw her arms around her best friend. "Sage! That's great!"

"Well," Sage said, stepping back and waving everyone inside, "maybe calling it a conversation is a bit of an exaggeration. I was asking her yes or no questions, and she was answering by sliding a book around."

Emily glanced over at Sage's huge desk and saw a slim volume sitting on it. "Still," Emily said, "that's progress for you."

"It is. Not only was Tessa answering me, but I was able to sense her presence. I might have disliked her in life, but being able to feel her ghost here with me was a massive relief. My abilities are beginning to recover. I even knew you were at the door, despite the fact none of you had made a sound."

Rylee and Vic were sitting shoulder-to-shoulder on the sofa, and Rylee was looking nervously around the room. "What did she tell you?" she asked Sage.

"Not much," Sage admitted. "Remember, right now, I'm basically just a ghost hunter instead of a medium. I can't communicate with Tessa the way I ordinarily would. However, I asked her if she knew her death was a murder, and she very clearly answered in the affirmative. I had asked her to push the book one way for yes and the opposite way for no. When I asked that question, she answered yes with such force that the book slid right off the edge of my desk."

"The question, then, is whether she knew before she died that someone was trying to kill her, or if she found out only after she became a ghost," Emily said.

"We already know the answer. I asked Tessa if she knew in life that someone wanted to kill her, and she gave me another yes. That means she must have figured out someone was poisoning her."

"But who?" Vic asked. He had one arm clamped around Rylee's shoulders, and Rylee seemed to be shrinking into herself.

Sage shrugged. "That, I don't know. I don't even think Tessa knows. She knew she didn't feel right, and I think she realized it wasn't just an ordinary illness but something being done to her intentionally. I think she died before she could figure out who was responsible."

"Poor Tessa," Rylee said, her voice not much above a whisper. "She must have been so terrified. She didn't even know who she could trust."

"Which is probably why she called me to pick her up on Monday," Sage said. "Tessa knew I didn't like her, but she also would have known that I hadn't been in the same places as her, which meant I couldn't be the one poisoning her."

"Can I please talk to Tessa?" Rylee asked. She glanced at Emily. "I need to apologize to her."

"Of course," Sage said. "We're going to stay with you, though. Anything Tessa shares could be useful information for the police. Where would you like to do this? You're welcome to use my consultation room."

Rylee pointed to a spot in the far corner. "I want to sit over there. I can feel a concentration of energy in that corner, and I think it might be Tessa."

Vic retrieved a chair from the consultation room. As Rylee instructed him where she wanted him to put it, Sage leaned toward Emily and whispered, "I'm looking forward to watching her in action. I want to see how her alleged abilities compare to Tessa's."

"She's been talking to the dark entity," Emily said, not bothering to whisper. "I think Rylee is a better psychic medium than Tessa ever was."

There were three quick banging noises right behind Emily, and she whirled around to see three books on the floor, right at her heels.

"Such a diva," Sage said, bending down to pick up the books. "At least she didn't actually hit you with them." When Sage stood back up, she narrowed her eyes at Emily. "What do you mean, Rylee has been talking to the entity? She's actually trying to communicate with it?"

"Yes, and that's the only reason I was able to talk to Scott. Rylee kept the entity busy so Scott felt safe coming out of hiding. Scott and Rylee both sense that there might still be some of the little girl she once was hiding under all that anger and aggression. I think she needs our help as much as Scott."

Sage poked Emily's arm. "After Rylee chats with her mentor, you and I are going to chat about that entity."

"I should have told you all of that already, but I was so excited about seeing Scott that the rest slipped my mind. Plus, things have been"—Emily gestured toward the corner, where Rylee was shooing Vic away from her—"chaotic."

"Rylee, do you want all of us to stand near you, or do you need space?" Sage called.

"I'd like you all to be close, but not too close," Rylee said, eyeing Vic significantly.

Emily, Sage, and Vic formed a semi-circle around Rylee, who sat down in the chair and took several deep breaths. Emily had expected her to close her eyes in concentration, but instead, Rylee tilted her head up and gazed at the ceiling. "Tessa, I know you're here. Will you please come talk to me?"

A planter with a fern in it slid off a small table that sat against the wall behind Rylee. The blue and red pottery shattered, and dirt sprayed across the floor.

"Really?" Sage grumbled.

"I'm sorry," Rylee said, her eyes wide. "I think that's my fault. Tessa might be mad at me."

"Tessa," Sage called, "I don't care who you're mad at. Please stop breaking my stuff."

In response, a box of tissues on the table slid off.

"Much better," Sage said.

"Thank you, Tessa," Rylee continued. "We're glad you're here. First, I want to apologize to you. I feel so horrible about our conversation on Sunday night, and I'm sorry about those things I said."

Sage leaned toward Emily until her lips were nearly against Emily's ear. "What did she say?"

"The F-word," Emily whispered back.

"Bad idea."

Emily just nodded in response as Rylee continued trying to coax Tessa into communicating through some method other than sliding objects off the table like some kind of spectral cat.

After ten minutes of making suggestions for other things Tessa could try, pleading for her cooperation, and, eventually, downright begging, Rylee's pinched expression relaxed, and a slight smile played at the corners of her lips. "I see it, Tessa," she said airily. "I can see it!"

"What do you see?" Sage asked.

"The old mill where we were filming on Monday. I see one of the crew guys pointing his camera at me. It's like I'm looking at the world through Tessa's eyes."

"Just like you experienced with the dark ent—with Lily," Emily said. "And like I experienced with Tessa yesterday."

"She's channeling her memory through you." Sage sounded impressed. "That's great. Does she have any memories that might indicate who had a big enough grudge to kill her?"

Rylee's face was still pointed toward the ceiling, but her eyes rolled up in her head, showing the whites. It gave Emily the creeps, especially when Rylee began narrating what she was seeing in a voice that sounded distant and detached.

"I'm talking and pointing at the old building behind me… I'm taking off the body mic… I just handed the mic to Steven, and he said something, but Tessa's not sending sound, just images… I'm sitting in a folding chair under the pop-up canopy the crew set up… I'm looking at my face—Tessa's face—in a compact mirror… I'm touching up my makeup… I'm reaching for a bottle of water… Oh! Now I'm looking at my phone. Brian is calling…"

Rylee fell silent, and Emily realized she, Vic, and Sage were all leaning toward Rylee anxiously. Had Tessa channeled that memory through Rylee for the express purpose of showing them Brian had called? Was that a suggestion that he might have had a motive for killing her?

"Why would he kill his own girlfriend, though?" Sage said.

"I was just wondering the same thing." Emily winked at Sage. "You read my mind."

"Tessa, please, why are you showing me that memory? What does it mean?" Rylee begged. Her eyes, Emily was relieved to see, had returned to their normal spots in their sockets.

"Please, Tessa, I need you to show me more. I don't

understand." Rylee reached up with both hands. "I want to help you."

Emily began to feel a strange sensation, almost a soft tickling feeling against her face and arms. Vic was glancing down at himself, and Emily knew he must be getting the same sensation.

Rylee's arms were still above her head, but she slowly rotated her wrists until her palms were facing upward in a warding-off gesture. "Tessa?"

Emily felt Sage's hand clamp onto her arm, and when Sage began backing away, Emily had no choice but to follow. She was about to ask what was going on when Sage sidestepped to put the sofa between herself and Rylee. "Get down!" Sage hissed.

Emily and Sage both crouched down as a thundering bang echoed through the room. The floor shuddered beneath Emily's feet, and books rattled on the shelves.

"Wow," Sage said. She released Emily's arm and stood slowly. "Everybody okay?"

Emily stood up, too, and she instantly saw that Rylee, at least, was not okay. She was sprawled face down on the floor in front of the chair, motionless.

"Rylee!" Vic cried. He appeared to have fallen onto his back, and he twisted around so that he could crawl on his hands and knees toward Rylee. "Hey, talk to me! Are you okay?"

"Oww…" was all Rylee managed.

Sage laughed nervously. "At least she's not dead."

"What just happened?" Emily asked.

"Tessa built up a huge amount of energy, then released it all at once. Like a psychic bomb." Sage scanned the room. "At least nothing else seems to be broken."

"Why would she do that?" Emily was talking to Sage, but she kept her eyes fixed on Rylee, who was slowly sitting up with Vic's help.

"Because she's a dramatic diva?" Sage suggested. She laughed, then said in a serious tone, "Honestly, Em, I don't know. She was communicating with me just fine earlier. Maybe Tessa is still mad at Rylee, and she let her anger build up until it burst like a dam."

"Whoa!" Vic said. Rylee had gotten to her feet, then toppled over, landing hard on her knees.

Sage and Emily both rushed forward to help Vic lift Rylee again, making sure she was settled in the chair before letting go.

"My legs feel like spaghetti," Rylee said. She closed her eyes as her chin drooped forward onto her chest. "I think Tessa built up all that energy by draining mine. I'm exhausted."

"You're welcome to take a nap on my sofa," Sage suggested.

"I think she'll be more comfortable in a bed," Vic said. "If you two can help me get her to the car, we should go back to Eternal Rest."

Emily hesitated, then nodded. She had promised Danny they would steer clear of Eternal Rest until he learned whether or not Brian was a suspect in Steven's murder. Still, it had been long enough that, surely, Brian was already at the station being questioned.

"Okay," Emily said eventually. "Sage, you're not going to stay here, are you? If Tessa is angry, I'm afraid she might do something even more harmful."

"I'm not giving up now! I'll ask Jen to bring her laptop over and work from here for the afternoon. She'll keep an eye on me."

"I was hoping we could all grab lunch, but Rylee clearly needs rest first," Emily said. "Let's see if we can get her down the stairs without all of us losing our balance."

Sage chuckled. "There's an elevator here, you know.

It's tiny and old, and it shudders so hard that you'll think you're about to plunge to your death, but it works."

Emily was grateful for the elevator, no matter how rickety it might be. Getting Rylee down the hall was tough enough. Rylee and Vic filled the little elevator, so Sage and Emily walked downstairs to meet them. While Rylee sat on a bench outside, Vic retrieved his car and pulled up right in front of her.

Once Rylee was in the car, Emily turned and caught Sage in a tight hug. "Be careful."

"You, too."

Emily tried to call Danny on the drive back to Eternal Rest. The call went to voicemail, so she told him they were heading back and expressed her wish that he was having better luck than her.

Rylee claimed she was feeling slightly better by the time Vic pulled up in front of Eternal Rest, so Emily volunteered to walk her up the front porch steps while Vic parked. Rylee was moving slowly, and she kept one hand on the stair railing and the other on Emily's forearm, but she was definitely getting some of her strength back.

Emily opened the front door and steered Rylee through it. As they crossed the threshold, a voice drifted from the dining room. "I dated her for six months. Of course I know her secrets! In fact, I watched her do that channeling trick so many times that I can do it the exact same way!"

21

Emily froze when she realized it was Brian's voice coming from the dining room. Had Danny already questioned Brian and cleared him of suspicion, or had they come back too soon?

While Emily was thinking about quietly backing out the front door and returning to Oak Hill, Rylee lurched forward and braced herself against the dining room doorway. "What are you talking about?" she shouted. "Did you steal Tessa's secrets?"

Emily crept closer and peered over Rylee's shoulder so she could see Brian. He said something quietly into his phone, then threw it down onto the dining room table, where it skittered to the far side. "You mean the secrets she refused to share with you?" he asked.

Emily jerked backward at the anger and bitterness in Brian's words. He had never struck her as overly nice, even when he had shown up on her doorstep with roses for Tessa, but the look on his face now was downright threatening.

While Emily felt intimidated by Brian's tone and look, Rylee seemed ready to rise to the challenge. Her voice was just as biting as Brian's. "Those secrets were how Tessa faked her mediumship abilities. I didn't need to know them, because I'm not a fake."

"You're just jealous that she shared more with me than with you," Brian sneered. "She never respected you."

"Why do you care about her tricks, anyway?"

"That's my business, not yours."

Rylee stepped back, bumping into Emily's shoulder and swaying slightly. Emily quickly put an arm around Rylee's waist to keep her steady. Any energy she had recovered during the drive back to Eternal Rest had been expended in her exchange with Brian. Rylee's face looked angry, but there was also a sadness in her expression as she asked, "Did you even love her?"

"Of course not! How could anybody love a narcissist like her? I just wanted to learn her methods."

Emily was on the verge of asking why Brian would want to do that when Rylee shouted, "So you learned her secrets, then killed her? Is that what you did, Brian?"

"Okay," Emily said in a firm voice. Even as she spoke, Brian's lips drew back, and his shoulders rounded forward. Emily thought wildly that he looked like an angry bull about to charge, and she pulled Rylee out of the doorway. "We need to go, Rylee. Right now."

"But—"

Emily turned and saw Vic standing at the front door. He still had one hand on the knob, and his other was covering his mouth, like he was trying not to cry out. Emily pointed out the door. "Go!"

Vic didn't question the order. He spun on his heel and nearly ran down the porch steps. Whatever the relationship between himself and Rylee might be, he seemed a lot more concerned with his own safety than hers at the moment.

Emily was getting Rylee out the front door as quickly as she could when she looked up and saw that even as Vic was hurrying toward his car, Danny was rushing toward the house.

"Emily," Danny said as he came to a stop right in front of her.

Between that single word and his expression, Emily understood everything that was going through his mind. She should have checked in with him before heading back to the house instead of just leaving a voicemail. She had possibly put herself and her guests in danger, and she had nobody to blame but herself. And, more than anything, Emily could sense Danny's concern for her. All of those thoughts flashed through her mind in a heartbeat, and without even thinking about it, Emily reached out and took Danny's hand, giving it a reassuring squeeze.

"We're okay," Emily said quickly. "Brian is in the dining room. He just admitted that he never loved Tessa. He was dating her to learn how she was faking her mediumship abilities."

Danny's expression of concern changed to one of curiosity, and he shot a glance over Emily's shoulder into the house. "Why would he want to know those things?"

"He wouldn't tell us. Where do you want us to go while you question him?"

"I don't want you to go anywhere. I'm afraid to let you wander off at this point." Danny tried to give Emily a playful smile, but combined with his nervous expression, it came off like more of a grimace. "I'll talk to Brian in the dining room. You and your guests sit tight. I had intended to make him come to the station, but when I called him earlier, he said he had left his car at Sutter's last night and had no way to get into Oak Hill."

Danny walked past Emily and into the dining room. As he closed the door behind him, Rylee shouted, "You may as well confess now, you heartless jerk!"

The front door and the parlor door both slammed shut.

"Danny and Brian are the only people inside the

house, and they're both in the dining room," Emily noted. "That means those doors were slammed by a ghost. I think your shouting might be upsetting one of my residents."

"It's that scary girl, Lily." Rylee sounded confident in her pronouncement. "I have no mentor and no TV show anymore, so I may as well work on helping you. If you can prop me up in my bed, I'll try communicating with Lily again."

"No," Emily said immediately. "You're exhausted after what Tessa did to you, and I don't think you're in the right mental state to talk to Lily. You need to be calm and focused to deal with her, not angry and sad."

"I disagree," Rylee said thoughtfully. "Maybe I can make Lily see that I'm upset, too. The people I was counting on are being taken away from me, just like Scott was taken away from her so many years ago. If I can show her that I have those kinds of feelings, too, but I'm willing to face them and work through them, then maybe I can convince her to work on her own anger and disappointment."

"It could be dangerous."

"I'll ask Vic to sit with me. He watched over Tessa many times when she was communicating with dangerous entities." Rylee laughed self-consciously. "Real entities, not made-up ones. He'll know what to do if things get bad. While I'm keeping Lily busy, you can try to make contact with Scott."

"Thank you, Rylee. I'll help you up to your room." Emily glanced at Vic, who had finally stopped and was standing next to his car, looking toward Rylee and Emily expectantly. Emily waved him over, then turned to escort Rylee upstairs. She was uncertain whether allowing Rylee to communicate with Lily was entirely safe, but Rylee's logic made sense. And, if Vic really knew how to keep

Rylee safe from an angry ghost, then everything would be okay.

Hopefully.

By the time Emily had gotten Rylee up the stairs and onto her bed, Vic had caught up to them. Emily wished Rylee luck with all her heart, then left as Rylee began outlining her plan to Vic.

Emily walked slowly to the parlor. Everything felt surreal. In one room, one of her guests was trying to have a conversation with the ghost that had killed Scott. In another room, Danny was talking to a man who might have killed one, if not two, people.

And I'm about to find out if the ghost of my husband is hanging around. This might be the strangest day I've ever had at Eternal Rest.

Emily sank down onto the sofa and tried to clear her mind. It was buzzing with everything that had happened in the past few days. She also tried to forget what Rylee and Danny were both doing so she could focus on her own conversation.

"Scott, are you here?" Emily asked. She called out to him several times, but there was no response and no feeling of his presence in the room with her. "Mrs. Thompson, are *you* here?"

There was a firm knock on the wall by the door.

"Is Scott here in the house?"

Two knocks told Emily that no, Scott was elsewhere.

"Is he in the—" Emily caught herself before she could give away Scott's hiding place, just in case Lily was listening in on her instead of communicating with Rylee. "Is Scott in his usual spot?" she asked instead.

Mrs. Thompson knocked once, but it was slightly hesitant. Emily took it to mean "I think so."

"Thanks, Mrs. Thompson. I'll go look for him there." Emily decided that a walk through Hilltop Cemetery might be just what she needed, anyway. Putting some distance between herself and everything happening in the house at the moment might make her feel more calm, and the fresh air wouldn't hurt, either.

There was just one car in the grass parking area between the cemetery and the road, and as Emily walked through Hilltop's iron gate, a jogger passed by on the brick walkway, giving her a friendly wave on their way out. Emily continued straight until she was about halfway up the hill, then turned right onto one of the concentric paths that ringed the hill. The Eisen mausoleum was on the north side of the cemetery, not far from the road, and by the time Emily reached it, the jogger had gotten in their car and left. Emily was the only living person left inside Hilltop Cemetery.

The Eisen mausoleum was a huge structure made of granite blocks. The top had a pyramid shape, and Emily could easily understand why the ghost of the drummer who had taken up residence there said he liked the acoustics. On the few occasions Emily had actually been inside the mausoleum, she had noticed the way her voice echoed up through the pyramid.

The front doors were secured with a thick chain that was padlocked around the handles, so Emily curled her fingers around the ironwork that fronted the window in one of the doors. "Scott," she called. "Rylee is trying to talk to Lily, so it should be safe for you to come out. Are you here?"

Scott answered from somewhere over Emily's left shoulder. "Why don't we sit here to talk?"

Emily turned and saw Scott's form shimmering on one end of a bench underneath an oak tree. Even though he was sitting in the shade, the bright daylight made him look much more translucent than he had inside the parlor. Emily walked over and sat down next to him, feeling a sting of sadness. Scott had always been strong, and he had always been the one to encourage Emily when business at Eternal Rest wasn't good. He had kept her going, and seeing him as just a wisp of his former self physically hurt. Emily reminded herself that his will was as strong as it had ever been, and what he looked like—or the fact he no longer had a corporeal body—didn't matter.

"Hey, Mr. Buchanan," Emily said softly.

"Hi there, Mrs. Buchanan." Scott and Emily smiled at each other, enjoying the formal address they had started using playfully with each other after a guest had insisted on calling them that.

"You know, I've been to your grave over at Oak Hill Memorial Garden so many times," Emily said. "I would talk to you, even though I knew your spirit wasn't there with me. It's nice that you can actually talk back now."

Scott gazed at the headstones and mausoleums around them, many half-hidden by the summertime growth of bushes and flowers. "It's a shame I couldn't have been interred here. It's so much prettier, and I would be right next door to you."

"It is too bad the city doesn't allow burials here anymore, but Reed makes sure your plot looks nice over at The Garden."

"Tell him I said thank you."

"I will."

"And please tell my mom thank you, too, and that I love her," Scott said. "It was so good to see her when she and her coven were here, and I know their magic is what allowed me to get through the barrier."

"She was excited to see you, too, and I know it made her feel good to help you."

"Do you think your psychic guest will be able to help Lily?" Scott asked, leaning forward to rest his elbows on his knees.

"That's our hope. Rylee is going to try to connect with

Lily by showing her that even though you suffer a loss, you can't let it define you."

"Good." Scott nodded. "If Lily can connect with a living person and feel some genuine empathy, then maybe she'll drop that shield of anger. She needs to cross over. I don't think I'll be at peace until she does."

"That makes sense," Emily agreed. "She's the one who killed you and has been keeping you weak. Once she's gone, you'll be safely inside the psychic barrier. There won't be any other entities for you to worry about. You'll get along great with Kelly, and you already know Mrs. Thompson."

Scott sat up straighter and looked at Emily with surprise. "When I say at peace, Emily, I mean truly at peace. Once Lily crosses over, then my business here will be done. It will be time for me to cross over, too."

Emily felt her breath catch in her throat. "But I just got you back. Aren't you going to stay with me?"

"No, Emily. I'm not."

Emily took a shaky breath. "Scott, please. I love you. I don't want you to leave."

"I love you, too, Emily, which is exactly why I need to cross over. You've been looking for me for nearly three years. I'm afraid that if I stayed with you, you would never move on."

"I don't want to lose you again."

Scott reached a hand toward one of Emily's, but his fingers simply slid right through hers. "Old habit, I guess." He smiled sadly as he retracted his hand. "And you won't be losing me again. You'll simply be letting me go. You and I have both earned some peace and quiet. Besides, you don't need me to stick around."

"I'll always need you, Scott." Emily could feel tears running down her cheeks, but she didn't care.

"No, you won't. You're so strong, Emily, and you've proven that in the time that I've been gone. Plus, you have amazing friends who support you and love you." Scott glanced in the direction of Eternal Rest. "There's even someone inside the house right now who loves you as more than a friend. I can feel it from here."

Emily averted her eyes in surprise and embarrassment. That was simply not a subject she felt comfortable discussing with Scott. She still thought of him as her husband, even if he was a ghost. Plus, even though she knew Danny was interested in her romantically, she had never gotten the impression that he loved her. Scott was clearly tapping into something Emily couldn't sense.

"He's a nice guy, but I'm not interested in seeing anyone," Emily said awkwardly.

"Maybe not right now, but once I'm gone, you'll reach a point where you're ready." Scott made a noise that was part laugh, part sigh. "Believe me, I don't really like the idea, either, but I don't want you to be alone, Emily. You deserve to be loved."

The image of Scott flickered and faded so much Emily could barely see him, even though he was right next to her on the bench. "My energy is fading," he said. "I need to recharge. Cross Lily over, and then I can follow. Please, Emily. Give me peace."

Scott disappeared with that final word, and Emily felt a cold, gentle breeze caress her face. Once the warm summer air removed any trace of the cold, she could sense that she was alone again.

Emily sat on the bench for a long time, her eyes staring at the Eisen mausoleum even though what she was seeing were memories of her life with Scott. His bright smile, the way he made her laugh with his silly puns, how he had talked about renovating the barn behind Eternal Rest into a house for themselves so they would have space for kids' bedrooms.

And now he was telling her to move on and love someone else.

"It's not that easy, Scott," Emily whispered. A part of her felt guilty because she knew Scott was right. She couldn't grieve his death for the rest of her life. At some point, she had to put the past behind her and open herself up to new things. New people. At the moment, though, Scott's story wasn't in the past. It was a huge part of her present, and as much as it might hurt, Emily knew the right thing to do was to honor his wish of having peace.

Eventually, Emily dried her eyes on the sleeve of her shirt and stood slowly. She ran her hands over her hair, making sure her low ponytail was still neat, and wiped a few bits of moss from her black jeans. *I'm not going to be any help to Scott if I just sit out here forever,* she told herself firmly.

As Emily rounded the hill on her walk back to Eternal Rest, she looked up and saw there were several cars parked alongside Vic's sedan and Danny's pick-up truck. She recognized them as belonging to Sage, Reed, and Trish. Emily had been walking slowly, mulling over her conversation with Scott, but her curiosity and concern that there was some kind of emergency made her quicken her pace.

The parlor was packed. In addition to Sage, Reed, and Trish, Emily also found Jen and Trevor waiting for her. Jen had a tray balanced in one hand, and she was handing glasses of sweet tea around. "I've got one for you, too," she said, turning to hand Emily a glass the second she crossed from the hallway into the parlor.

Emily accepted the tea gratefully, but instead of drinking it, she raised the cold glass to her forehead. It felt both physically and mentally soothing. When she lowered it, she said, "No one told me I was hosting a party."

"Sage just called and said to get over here as quick as I could," Reed said. "I told her I would have to take off work early, and she said to do it."

"And Sage and Jen showed up at my work and told me I was coming with them, period," Trevor added. "I'm not even sure why we're here."

"Me, neither," Trish said. She looked at Sage with raised eyebrows. "You said we had to wait until Emily got here before you'd explain, and Emily's here now, so spill it. What kind of spooky mission are we on?"

Sage spread her hands and gave a little shrug. "I don't

know. I just suddenly got this feeling that we needed to be here, and it felt urgent. Something told me Emily needed her friends with her. Maybe I'm psychic!"

"I was just having a conversation with Scott, and he told me my friends love me." Emily looked around at everyone seated or standing in her parlor and felt a wave of warmth rush through her. "He was right. Y'all are the best."

"You've been talking to Scott?" Reed asked, sounding impressed.

"Yeah, and he says thanks for keeping his plot looking good."

"What else did he say?" Trish asked. Her eyes were wide with excitement. "Does he miss my biscuits? I bet he does!"

Before Emily could answer, she heard the sound of the dining room door opening behind her. She turned and saw Danny, who looked grim. Emily stepped aside so he could join them in the parlor. At the same time, she saw Brian walk out the front door. His head was down, and his shoulders were hunched.

"He's not in handcuffs, I see," Emily said.

"No, because he's not the one who killed Steven Bates. I've been holding him in the dining room until we could confirm his alibi. I just got the call that Brian was telling me the truth."

"And that truth is…?" Jen prompted. She handed Danny the last glass of iced tea on her tray.

"He left Sutter's the night of Steven's murder because he met a woman and went home with her. He was at her place until about midnight, when she called a cab to bring him back here because he was so drunk he could barely walk. Both the woman and the cab driver have verified Brian's story. We even have a copy of the credit card receipt from the cab driver. It's time stamped just a few minutes before Brian showed up on your security camera footage, Emily."

"Brian could still be the one who killed Tessa," Sage pointed out.

Danny sighed wearily. "You're right. At this point, though, we have a lot of suspects but zero evidence against any of them. Vic, Rylee, Brian, the show's crew members, even Bernie Moss. And, of course, there are other people from Tessa's life who could have poisoned her, since we know it was happening before she ever got to Oak Hill. Brian even said Tessa hadn't been feeling well for the past few weeks, and she was having to use extra makeup to make herself appear healthy."

"Since she died here in Oak Hill, don't you think it's likely her killer followed her here?" Emily asked. "That way, they could continue poisoning her."

"Yes, I think it's likely our killer is either someone here in town for the TV show or our overly enthusiastic protestor." Danny shook his head. "At the same time, now that Steven Bates has also been murdered, I'm worried any one of our suspects could become the next victim."

"Sage, did Tessa communicate any more with you this afternoon?" Emily asked.

"She threw more books onto the floor."

Jen frowned. "She didn't really throw them. It's more like she slid them off the shelves."

"Which means Tessa wasn't doing it out of anger, but because she wanted to communicate something with it," Emily speculated.

"That's the feeling I got." Jen shrugged. "But then, I'm not a psychic medium."

"Jen makes a good point," Sage said. "I'm biased toward Tessa, so I took the falling books as an expression of anger or displeasure. But it was different than the previous times."

"She had you drive her to a bookstore," Trevor said to Sage. "And, now, she's using books to get your attention. Maybe there's something in the books she wants you to see."

"Or in the books she was looking at during her visit to Under the Covers," Danny added. "We did consider that the books had some hidden meaning, but they didn't really make sense. Not even Tessa's ghost can give us a solid lead."

Trish laughed wryly. "We need a lead for lead poisoning. Isn't it funny how those words are spelled the same but pronounced differently?"

Emily gasped. "You're right, Trish! Danny, what were the titles of the books Tessa left out at the bookstore? Wasn't one of them about history's leaders, or something?"

Danny pulled his notebook out of his pocket and began riffling through the pages. "*To Lead with Purpose: Notable Figures of the 19th Century.*"

Sage was so excited she jumped up from the sofa. "To lead! You think Tessa was trying to leave a message that she was being poisoned with lead, and that title was the closest thing she could find?"

"Maybe," Emily said. She put her iced tea down on a side table and began to drum her fingertips together. "I think Tessa figured out she was being poisoned. She made a list of her symptoms—the headaches, the stomach issues, the way she looked—and realized what was happening to her. Once she knew she was being poisoned, I bet she started doing research and learned it was likely lead poisoning. Tessa might have known she was dying, so she put those books out to tell us what was causing it."

"Wait a minute," Trevor said, raising a hand. "Wouldn't she have simply gone to a hospital for treatment? Or gone to the police?"

"It's possible she only figured it out there at the bookstore," Jen noted. "Maybe she realized she was being poisoned, then went to Seeing Beyond to ask Sage for help."

"That threatening note might have been Tessa's killer acknowledging Tessa was onto them," Danny said. "If Tessa had figured out someone was intentionally making her sick, the person doing it might have threatened her so she wouldn't tell anyone. And they might have followed her to make sure she stayed quiet."

"And Tessa probably thought she was being followed, so she would have been afraid to go to the authorities," Trevor said. "What Bernie and Trish both said about Tessa's behavior when she stopped into Grainy Day on her way to Sage's backs that up. If she was worried someone was tailing her and would prevent her from making it to Sage's, let alone the hospital or police station, she might have left clues to help us track down her killer. And, don't forget, she was psychic. She might have known she didn't have much time left."

"Psychic or not, Tessa still wasn't sure who was trying to kill her, so she would have been afraid to confide in anyone. She may have left her cell phone at the bookstore because she didn't want her killer to be able to track her down with it," Emily pointed out. "Danny, what were the other books Tessa left sitting out at Under the Covers?"

"*Fashion Through the Ages* and *Quack Cures and Snake-Oil Salesmen*," Danny read.

"What do fashion and quack cures have to do with lead poisoning?" Trish wondered.

"Maybe that last title was self-referential," Sage said with a snicker. "Tessa was a bit of a snake-oil salesman."

"Sage, she's dead!" Trish pressed a hand against her heart.

"Sorry, I forgot you're a fan. But it was kind of funny."

Trish just rolled her eyes and made a noise of disgust.

Meanwhile, Emily was already walking toward her laptop. She plopped down into her chair and typed the title of the fashion book into a search engine. A link to the publisher's site came up as the first result, so she clicked on it and began to read the book's description. When she finished, she sat back and said, "Ohhh."

"Em?" Sage asked.

Emily spun around in her chair. "Danny, how did the lead wind up inside Tessa?"

"Probably in her food. We're waiting on lab results."

"I don't think she ate the lead." Emily stood. "You just said Tessa started looking so bad that she had to pile on extra makeup. That fashion book was about clothing and makeup, and the description mentions toxic formulas for cosmetics."

"Of course," Jen said. "I remember reading about how lead was once a main ingredient in face powder, hundreds of years ago. It was also used in so-called medicines, which explains the quack cures book."

"Tessa was trying to narrow down how the poison was getting into her system," Danny said, nodding. "If someone was putting it in her makeup, she was getting low-level lead poisoning every time she put it on. When she started wearing more makeup to hide how ill she looked, she also started getting more lead in her system."

"She inadvertently killed herself with her own vanity." This time, there was no trace of humor in Sage's voice. Instead, she sounded horrified.

When Emily spoke again, her voice was barely above a whisper. "I know exactly who killed Tessa, and I think I know why."

"It's been right there in front of me this whole time," Emily said. "The lead that you needed, Danny. It was such an offhand comment, though, that I had practically forgotten about it."

"Emily, tell us who killed Tessa before Sage explodes from anticipation," Reed said. Sage was twisted around on the sofa to get a good view of Emily, and she was bouncing up and down on the cushion, her fingers drumming the back of the sofa anxiously.

Danny pulled out his cell phone, one finger poised over the screen. "Where do I need to send officers?"

"Nowhere. He's here." Emily turned her head upward, in the direction of room number three. "Vic killed Tessa."

Danny shut the parlor door as the room fell into silence. For a moment, Emily thought her friends were simply stunned by her cleverness. Then, Trish said incredulously, "Tessa's assistant? Why in the world would he want her dead?"

"Vic was right there in my office with Tessa's ghost," Sage noted. "Why didn't she attack him?"

"I thought he worshipped the ground she walked on," Trevor said. "That's what you made it sound like, at least."

"Vic adored Tessa," Emily agreed. "But I'm almost

certain there's someone he adores even more, and that's Rylee. He might have been upset that she was always in Tessa's shadow."

"Oh," Sage said. "I thought I was getting a romantic vibe from those two when they were at Seeing Beyond."

"On Monday night," Emily began, "when we were wondering where Tessa could be, Vic said he had just gotten back from the Atlanta area because Tessa sent him there to buy some specialty makeup that she liked. He was complaining about having to go so far for it. If part of his job as her assistant was to buy her makeup, then he could have been adding lead to it. It would have been so easy for him to do. And to your point, Sage, even if that book helped Tessa realize it might have been her makeup that was poisoned, I doubt she would have suspected Vic. He acted like he lived to make her happy."

"Emily, you're coming upstairs with me. The rest of you stay in this room." Danny spoke like a parent trying to keep kids in line. "Shut the door after us, and do not come out for any reason."

Trish and Sage looked disappointed, and Jen looked frightened. Reed, as unruffled as ever, simply drawled, "Good luck."

Danny outpaced Emily heading up the stairs, and by the time she caught up with him, he was already knocking on the door to Vic's room. There was no answer, so Emily pointed at Rylee's room. "He might still be in there, with Rylee."

Rylee answered the door when Danny tried knocking on that one, and she looked even more exhausted than before. "Something's wrong," she blurted as soon as she saw Danny and Emily.

"Yes," Danny answered grimly.

"How do you know already? He just started acting like

this a few minutes ago." Rylee stepped back and gestured toward Vic, who was sitting on the far side of the bed. He was bent forward at the waist, and he was clutching the sides of his head.

Danny swept past Rylee and stood in front of Vic. He peered at him for a moment, then said, "Vic, are you okay?"

"It's all going wrong," Vic said, not even looking up.

"He keeps saying that over and over again," Rylee said. She was leaning against the wall, and her mascara was running down her pale, pinched face.

"How long has this been going on?" Emily asked.

"He started acting strange while I was communicating with Lily, and it just got worse and worse. He won't even respond to me."

"Vic Orman," Danny said loudly, "did you kill Tessa Valentine?"

Vic finally looked up at Danny, though his hands remained clamped against his head. "It wasn't supposed to happen this way!"

"What wasn't supposed to happen this way, Vic?" Danny's voice was softer, and he perched on the edge of the antique rocking chair that sat next to the bed. He sounded like he was trying to comfort a friend. "Did you realize you were going to get caught?"

Vic brought his hands down and grabbed fistfuls of the bedspread. "I never meant to kill Tessa in the first place!" His shoulders shook as he choked back a sob.

"But you were putting lead in her makeup, weren't you?" Danny said.

"Yes, but not enough to kill her!"

"If you weren't trying to kill her, then why did you do it in the first place?"

"Because," Vic wailed, "I wanted to make her too sick

to film the show so Rylee could be the star instead." He turned and looked imploringly at Rylee. "I'm so sorry. I didn't mean to kill Tessa. I just wanted her out of the way. I wanted you to get the attention and fame you deserve!"

Rylee stared at Vic as she groped toward Emily. She gripped Emily's hand, then slowly began to slide down the wall. Emily helped ease her into a seated position on the floor.

"I started adding the lead a few months ago, once the contracts for the TV show had been signed," Vic explained. "I knew Tessa would never let Rylee share the spotlight, so I looked for a way to make her sick enough that she couldn't work. I remembered that lead used to be put in makeup and could sometimes be absorbed into the skin. I did a bunch of research and found the right chemical formula for getting lead to sink into the skin, and then I started playing with how much to put in her makeup."

"You experimented on her?" Rylee cried.

"I had to," Vic said. "I had to figure out the right amount. Tessa would sometimes feel fine, so I would know I wasn't using enough, but I didn't want to use so much she wound up having to go to the hospital. When we started filming on Monday, I could tell she was feeling bad. There was no way she was going to be able to keep up a busy filming schedule all week. Still, she wasn't supposed to actually die!"

Emily was crouching down next to Rylee, who was still clutching her hand. Emily met Danny's eyes, though her words were directed at Vic. "What you didn't count on was that Tessa would have to use more and more makeup as she started looking worse," she said. "She was absorbing far more lead than you realized, day after day."

"And when you realized Tessa had begun to suspect someone was making her sick," Danny said, "you sent her that anonymous note. *If you tell, I tell.* You wanted her to be so afraid of having her fraudulent methods exposed that she wouldn't try to find out who was doing this to her, let alone seek help."

For the first time since they had come upstairs, Vic sounded almost like his normal self. He even sat up a little straighter. "I didn't write that note. That protester who follows Tessa around slipped it to her when we passed her after lunch on Monday. She was on the sidewalk outside the restaurant where we ate, along with her judgmental friends."

"What secret could Tessa have possibly known about Bernie?" Emily asked incredulously.

Vic gave a smug little laugh. "That Bernie Moss, little Miss Righteous, used to go to a psychic weekly. The psychic is a friend of Tessa's, and she spilled the beans. Tessa threatened to tell Bernie's friends, and Bernie retaliated with her own threat."

Danny and Emily exchanged a quick glance. Despite all of their speculation about it, the note hadn't actually been a clue to Tessa's murder, after all. Tessa, Emily realized, must have put it inside one of the books in the hopes that it would convince the police to put Bernie Moss on the suspect list, just in case she was the one poisoning Tessa. Emily wondered if Tessa had ever once considered that the person who was actually killing her slowly was her own assistant.

"If you wanted Rylee to be the star of the show, then why did you kill the show's producer?" Danny asked. The friendliness in his voice was gone. Since Vic was finally talking freely, Danny had returned to his usual detective demeanor.

"Oh, Vic, no," Rylee moaned.

Emily wanted to say the same thing. As soon as she had

read about lead historically being used in makeup, she had made the connection between Vic and Tessa's murder. She couldn't imagine why Vic would have wanted to kill Steven.

Vic had sounded so remorseful about killing Tessa, but he suddenly sounded angry as he shouted, "He was going to cancel the show, Rylee!"

"What? No, we were still filming."

"Yeah, but not for long. I met him at that bar, and by the time I got there, Steven was about four beers in. He started telling me that he was going to pull the plug on the show. He said Rylee didn't have the charisma to carry it, and he didn't want to waste any more time and money than he already had."

"You killed him just because he was going to cancel the show?" Emily asked.

"I didn't mean to! I got angry, and I left, but I realized that wouldn't solve anything, so I went back. I saw Brian's car in the parking lot, and I didn't want to talk about it in front of him, so I waited outside the bar all afternoon and evening. Brian left, and I just kept waiting. I wanted to speak to Steven privately, not in the middle of the bar. When Steven finally came out, I begged him to reconsider. He just brushed me off and started walking back to his hotel. I followed, still pleading with him, and he just kept ignoring me. I got so angry, and I just, I just... I couldn't help it! He was being so stupid!"

"Are you saying you strangled Steven to death, and that he deserved it?" Danny was looking at Vic as if he might be joking.

"Of course he deserved it! He was going to rob Rylee of her chance to be a famous psychic medium, just like Tessa!"

"Last night, you told us a car had tried to run you off

the road," Emily said. "You just made that up to explain why you were so shaken up, didn't you?"

"It's all going wrong," Vic said again, burying his face in his hands.

"And you're under arrest," Danny said. He stood and pulled out a pair of handcuffs. "Come on, Vic. You can confess everything all over again at the station."

Danny put Vic in handcuffs, and even after hearing their tread on the stairs and the bang of the front door closing behind them, Emily realized Rylee was still staring blankly at the spot Vic had been occupying on the bed.

"Rylee?" Emily said softly. She shifted so she was sitting on the floor, too. "I'm so sorry."

"How did I not realize something was wrong? I should have sensed something was off with Vic."

"He worked for Tessa. I'm sure he learned a long time ago how to block his mind from psychics."

"Yeah." Rylee leaned sideways until her head rested against Emily's shoulder. Emily could feel Rylee's body shaking as she began to cry. "I thought I was going to marry him someday!"

There was a loud bang, followed by a sound like splintering wood. Emily looked up just in time to see the tall maple dresser on the opposite wall tip forward. It crashed onto the floor as Emily and Rylee both leapt to their feet.

"Whoa!" Emily cried.

"It's her. Lily." Rylee rubbed her eyes. "I don't think she likes seeing me unhappy. She doesn't want me to feel the way she does."

"I know you're exhausted, Rylee," Emily began, "but if you have a connection with Lily, then you're the one who has the best chance of getting her to cross over."

There were loud footsteps in the hallway, and Trevor and Reed sprinted into the room.

"We heard a crash," Trevor said, his words running together.

"Are you okay?" Reed asked.

"Yeah, we're okay. The entity knocked over that dresser." Emily smiled wanly. "Thanks for ignoring Danny's command to stay put in the parlor."

"Maybe one of them can sit with me," Rylee said. "I think Lily still doesn't like you, Emily. She might be more willing to listen if you're not here, but I don't want to be by myself."

"You're going to communicate with the ghost?" Trevor asked. "I'll stay with you."

"Keep an eye on her," Emily said firmly. "If Lily can tip over a dresser, who knows what else she can do? Plus, Rylee is already exhausted."

Trevor put both hands on Emily's shoulders and looked at her earnestly. "We'll be okay. I promise."

As Reed and Emily walked down the stairs, Emily muttered, "That dresser was an antique."

"You're more upset about furniture than the fact Danny just marched a murderer out your front door?" Reed laughed. "I'm glad your priorities are in order."

"Like you said, Danny was taking him out, so Vic can't kill anyone else. I assume you were all spying out the front windows?"

Jen was standing in the hallway, and she answered, "Of course we were. Come tell us what happened."

Emily sank down into one of the wingback chairs and quickly recounted Vic's confession to two murders. "So that's it. You know, Rylee told me this town draws in ghosts and psychics, but sometimes I feel like Oak Hill is more of a magnet for murderers."

Reed was standing behind the sofa, and he shifted from one foot to the other. "She's not wrong, you know."

"Sure, we know ghosts were flocking here to get inside the psychic barrier before the witches strengthened it."

"No, it's not just about the psychic barrier." Reed looked slightly embarrassed as he continued, "There is a spiritual energy here, and mediums and people who are sensitive to the paranormal are drawn to it. When I left for college, I felt its absence."

24

"I knew it!" Emily nearly shouted in her excitement. At the same time, Sage said, "A-ha!"

"Yes, you have said for a long time now that you thought I had some kind of sixth sense," Reed said. He pointed a finger at Emily. "You were right."

"Why have you hidden it from us?" Sage asked. "I always knew you had something special, but I was never sure if you were a medium or just a sort of conduit for manifesting paranormal activity."

"I'm not quite sure how to define myself, either," Reed said. "I've always skirted the question of whether I have any abilities, because I'm not even sure what my abilities are. My family comes from the Lowcountry on the coast of Georgia, but my great-great-grandmother heard about this sort of energy vortex up in North Georgia, and she insisted on moving the entire family here. That was more than a century ago."

"She was a psychic medium, then," Sage speculated.

"And a root worker. She was a powerful woman, and even though I didn't get all of those supernatural genes, I did inherit some of her talents. It's one of the reasons I'm so rarely afraid of ghosts. They just seem like people to me, partly because that's how I was raised, and partly because I can sense them better than most people."

"I'm glad to know your abilities weren't just my imagination," Emily said with a smile.

"And your own growing mediumship abilities are probably tied to this energy vortex," Reed continued. "You've been advancing at an incredible pace, probably because of your proximity to it. I expect it's one of the reasons Scott moved to Oak Hill. Even though his mom had given him that necklace to block his psychic abilities, I think he must have been unconsciously drawn here."

"This is all making so much sense," Sage said. "When I left for college, I swore I was never coming back to this Podunk town, but I just kept getting this urge to make Oak Hill my home. I told myself my love for Oak Hill must have been stronger than I realized, but it makes a lot more sense that it's because I felt that energy, too, and I wanted to be close to it."

"And this energy might be able to help you recover your mediumship abilities," Jen said excitedly. "If we can find out where it's centered and take you there, I bet you'll be back to normal in no time!"

"Like she was ever normal to begin with," Reed said, grinning at Sage.

"All the ghosts coming to Oak Hill must feel the energy, too, so when the psychic barrier weakened, they came here not just to be safely inside the barrier, but also to be near the energy," Emily speculated.

"This also helps explain why a lot of the ghosts we've encountered are so powerful. They're feeding off that energy." Sage nodded happily. "This all feels like a revelation."

"Is this why you wanted us all to be here today, Sage?" Reed asked. "So I could reveal the secrets of my family and Oak Hill?"

Sage paused, tilting her head to one side as if she were

listening. "No, I think we came here to help Emily. And I think that moment has arrived."

Even as Sage spoke, Emily could hear slow footsteps on the stairs. A moment later, Rylee and Trevor came into the parlor. Rylee was leaning heavily on Trevor's arm, and Trish quickly jumped up from the sofa so Rylee could sit.

Rylee looked like she could barely sit up straight, but there was a small, satisfied smile on her lips. "She's ready. Lily says she'll cross over, but she has to do one thing first. She wants to apologize to Scott."

"Kelly?" Emily called to the room. "Can you please go to the Eisen mausoleum next door and ask Scott to join us?"

There was a knock on the wall, which Emily knew was Mrs. Thompson's way of saying Kelly was on her way.

Sage had just asked Rylee about her conversation with Lily when there was a flurry of knocking on the wall.

"Mrs. Thompson, is everything okay?" Emily asked, instantly worried.

One knock confirmed there was nothing to panic about.

"Are you telling us that Scott is here?"

Knock!

"Thanks, Mrs. T!" Sage was looking around the room. "This is so weird. I can tell the vibration in here is different, but I just can't sense Scott the way I should be able to. Still, this is the reason I wanted all of us here. Gang, it's going to take teamwork, but you've all done this before. Open yourselves up. Be willing to give your energy to Scott, and to Lily, for that matter. This is the moment Emily and Scott have been waiting for."

Sage's words felt oddly ominous to Emily, and she felt her chest tighten. It was true; it was the moment she had been waiting for, ever since Scott's car crash. She had always known, despite the lack of evidence, that his crash hadn't been normal, and she had always suspected his ghost was still on Earth and needed her assistance. Emily had never wanted anything more than to help Scott's ghost find peace, but in that moment, she realized she had never truly considered what that meant, and how much it was going to hurt. It was like losing him all over again.

Emily bit her lip to fight back her tears. "Scott?" she called, her voice shaking. "You heard Sage. Feel free to harness our energy, if you need to. Lily wants to talk to you, and we are all right here to help you and to keep you safe. It's okay."

There was a faint shimmer in the air between the two front windows, and Scott's ghost quickly materialized. Trevor gasped, and Trish shouted an expletive.

Scott laughed. "Nice to see you, too, Trish. I sure do miss your biscuits."

"I told you!" Trish said triumphantly to Emily.

"It's good to see all of you. Trevor, it's nice to meet you."

Trevor nodded his head, staring at Scott with wide eyes and his mouth slightly open.

"Scott, Lily is willing to cross over, but she wants to talk to you first," Emily said. She turned to Rylee. "Is she here?"

"Lily," Rylee called. "Come talk to Scott. We're all here to help you, so don't be afraid."

Suddenly, Reed whipped his head around, then stepped to the side. A little girl—transparent, but with a slightly dark halo around her—had appeared right behind him. She had long golden curls, and her ruffled gingham dress looked like something from the nineteenth century.

"Scott," Lily said in a high voice, "I'm sorry. You were my best friend, and when you stopped talking to me, I just got so angry. And I got angrier and angrier and angrier, and... well, I think I was so angry that I forgot how to be nice."

"I'm so sorry I hurt your feelings, Lily," Scott said gently. "Did Rylee explain to you what happened?"

"Yes, she told me your momma made it so you couldn't see me anymore. That was mean of her."

"She did it because I wasn't just seeing you, Lily. I was also seeing dark, scary things. She didn't even know about you. She was simply trying to keep me safe."

Lily looked at Scott thoughtfully, then nodded. "I understand. I'm sorry I got so angry, and I'm sorry I made you die. I just wanted you to stay with me."

"I know that. I am so proud of you for making the decision to cross over. You're going to find your family again, and you're going to be very happy."

"You should see them, Lily," Rylee said. "You'll see a bright light, and if you go toward it, you'll see all the people you love."

"Maybe I'll see you there," Scott added.

Lily smiled at Scott. "I would like that. I'll introduce you to my parents. They're very nice people." Lily's form began to fade. "Oh, I see it! It's so bright and beautiful! Momma?"

Lily disappeared, and a second later, Trevor sucked in his breath and pressed a hand against his chest. "Oh! I think she went right through me!"

"Since when can you sense ghosts?" Sage asked with a laugh. "Everyone but me is a psychic medium today!"

"She did it," Rylee said, leaning her head against the back of the sofa. "Lily has crossed over."

"She's finally at peace," Scott said, looking at Emily significantly. "And now it's time for both of us to have peace, too."

"I'm not ready," Emily said. Her face crumpled as she began to cry. She stood and moved so she was standing just a few inches in front of Scott. "I'm not ready for this."

"You are, Emily. Look around you. These people are your family and your future. They will be here for you, and I know I'm leaving you in good hands. I will always love you, Emily, and I know you will always love me, but this is the peace we both need. You won't have to worry about me anymore, and for me, the misery of being stuck between this world and the next will finally be over."

Emily wiped away the tears on her cheeks. There was a throbbing pain in her chest, as if her heart were actually breaking. She knew, though, that Scott was right. More importantly, it was what he wanted. It would be cruel of her to deny him the peace he was seeking.

"Goodbye, Scott," Emily said.

"Thank you for never giving up on me. You saved me." Scott lifted a hand, stopping just short of Emily's cheek, and she could feel the cold emanating from him. "I love you, Mrs. Buchanan."

Even though she was crying, Emily still smiled at the name. One last shared joke, one last smile for Scott. "I love you, too, Mr. Buchanan."

Scott blinked out of sight, and Emily felt a blast of cold air radiate from where he had been standing. She could feel that his presence was no longer in front of her.

Scott was gone.

Emily brought both hands up to her face and began to cry even harder. Vaguely, she felt arms encircle her. Her eyes were closed, but she could sense that her friends had crowded in around her, and she heard someone else openly crying.

As she stood there, surrounded by the people who loved her, Emily realized she felt a sense of calm. Scott had been right: she had been searching for peace since his death, just like him. Now, finally, Scott was at rest, and that meant Emily could be, too.

"There's still one thing I want to know. Why did Brian want to learn how Tessa faked some of her psychic abilities?" Sage asked.

Danny laughed. "Believe it or not, he wanted to open up his own business helping clients connect with their deceased loved ones, just like you. Brian said he's very good at reading people, but he doesn't have any supernatural talents. He dated Tessa so he could learn how she made it look so real."

Jen whistled. "Wow. Whatever I had expected, it was not that."

Emily hadn't said much since joining her friends for lunch at The Depot. She was content just to enjoy their company and to soak up the sun as they sat at two tables they had pushed together on the patio. Even Trevor and Reed were there, spending their lunch breaks to support Emily.

Because, even though Sage had said the lunch was to celebrate solving two murders, Emily knew it was really about rallying around her. It hadn't even been twenty-four hours since Scott had crossed over, and already it felt like some surreal dream.

"Speaking of Brian," Danny said, "I assume he and Rylee checked out this morning?"

"They did," Emily said. "I started the week with three guests. Of them, one was killed and the other was a killer. Rylee is the last guest standing."

"And Brian," Jen said.

"He wasn't even supposed to be a guest! He showed up to surprise Tessa for their six-month anniversary."

"The fraud boyfriend dating the fraud psychic," Sage mused. "What a week. You know, for a diva who loved putting on a show and getting a lot of attention, Tessa really turned out to be a little lackluster about helping us find clues."

"She helped a bit with the investigation," Emily pointed out. "The memories she channeled through Rylee included one of her touching up her makeup. It was a clue, and we completely ignored it."

"Yeah," Sage said grudgingly. "I guess I'm still a little bitter about her pelting us with books. I'm looking forward to crossing her over after lunch."

Emily noticed Reed and Trevor were huddled together at their end of the table. They were leaning close to each other and speaking in low tones, so Emily couldn't hear what they were saying, but she could see Reed gesturing impatiently.

"Okay," Emily called, "what are you boys gossiping about over there?"

Trevor instantly sat up and crossed his arms. "Nothing."

"You should tell her," Reed said.

"But—"

"Do it! You'll be glad you did."

Emily instantly flashed to the memory of Scott's ghost in the cemetery, telling her that there was someone inside Eternal Rest right then who loved her as more than a friend. She had assumed Scott meant Danny, since he had been in the dining room at the time, questioning Brian.

Suddenly, though, Emily was struck with the thought that by the time Scott had told her that, the rest of her friends had already arrived and were waiting for her in the parlor.

Had Scott been talking about Trevor instead of Danny? Was Reed urging him to confess his feelings for her right there in front of everyone?

Oh, no, no, no, please, no! Emily thought desperately. *I am not ready for this.*

Trevor sighed deeply and straightened his shoulders. "Emily, you mentioned something about me being out having fun on Saturday night. I think you assumed I was on a date."

No. No. Noooo!

"Well, actually, I was having dinner with a local witch."

Emily's eyebrows drew down in confusion. "What?"

"When that coven was staying with you, you asked for my help getting Evelyne alone so you could question her. I asked Serenity to give me some magical advice outside so you and Evelyne could have a private chat."

"I remember," Emily said slowly. She had no idea where Trevor's story was going, or how him talking to a witch tied in to him being in love with her.

"I asked Serenity how I could use magic to communicate with ghosts. I figured that if magic is all about energy, and ghosts are just energy, then there should be some way of using the one with the other. You know how important it is to me to help these ghosts get justice. By learning to communicate with them myself, I can be even more of a help, to them and to you."

Emily stared at Trevor in stunned silence. She had expected a confession of love, and what she had gotten instead was a confession of a completely different kind.

Out of the corner of her eye, Emily could see Sage, Jen, and Danny, their heads looking from one end of the table to the other as if they were watching a tennis match.

They, too, were silent, and Emily assumed they were as surprised as she was.

Emily was so relieved Trevor wasn't declaring his love for her that she just started laughing. When Trevor looked taken aback, she waved her hands. "No, I'm not laughing at you, Trevor," she said quickly, her laugh subsiding into a giggle. "It's been such a strange, stressful week, and I just didn't expect it to end with that news. I'm actually really excited for you. You've talked so much about finding a way to be more involved in murder investigations, and I half expected you to quit your job and join the police. But you found your own way to help ghosts. That's wonderful."

"I suspect the energy here in Oak Hill will help Trevor with his magic," Reed said. "He should make good progress."

"Good," Sage said, winking at Trevor. "He's always been clueless when it comes to the paranormal, so he can use all the help he can get. Who's the witch?"

"The friend of a co-worker. I met her at a get-together he had at his house, and we got to talking. I'm taking lessons from her, and on Saturday, I took her out to dinner. It was a way for me to say thanks, but we mostly did it because the restaurant is haunted, and she wanted to see if I could sense anything."

"Well, did you?" Reed asked.

"I think so, but I'm still not sure."

"Now there are four of us who can communicate with ghosts, or at least, there will be soon," Emily said, grinning. "Yes, Reed, I'm counting you. This is fantastic!"

"Before you all get too excited," Sage said in a warning tone, "remember, I'm the OP."

Jen wrinkled her nose. "The OP?"

"The original psychic."

Everyone at the table groaned.

"And I'm ready to prove to the world that my psychic

mediumship abilities are returning," Sage continued, ignoring everyone. "I'm going to cross Tessa Valentine. Em, I know you're willing to do it, but I would like to have that honor."

"It's all yours, Sage. I'll just come along for moral support."

"And to witness my triumphant comeback. Let's pay and get out of here so we can wrap up the final piece of this murder investigation!"

Emily hugged every one of her friends before setting off with Sage toward Seeing Beyond. Despite the August heat, the walk made Emily feel energized. Now that Scott was finally at rest, everything seemed to have a fresh new glow. The square in downtown Oak Hill had never looked so green and lush to Emily, and even the old buildings seemed prettier than ever. Even though she was still heartbroken about having to say goodbye to Scott, she was grateful that his spirit was no longer suffering. To Emily, it seemed like a sad, scary chapter of her life had been closed, and she could tell, in part, by the way the world around her looked.

"You seem happy," Sage commented as they walked along the sidewalk toward Seeing Beyond.

"I'm sad and happy," Emily said honestly.

"When Scott died, it was so sudden that you never got any closure. This time, you got to say goodbye."

Emily looked at her best friend and smiled. "I can see why you love helping people connect with their deceased loved ones. It must feel good to help others get that closure, too."

"It's the best job in the world."

"Nah, running Eternal Rest is the best job in the world."

Sage chuckled. "Your guests need to stop getting themselves killed, though, or your online reviews are going to tank."

"The dead can't leave reviews," Emily said, nudging Sage's arm playfully.

"And they can't hang out in my shop indefinitely. I'm proud that I get to be the one to send Tessa on her way. It's like I get the last word with her, and I get to prove to her once and for all that I'm an authentic psychic medium."

"I doubt Tessa ever really believed you were a fake. She probably sensed how powerful you are—"

"How powerful I was," Sage corrected.

"And will be again. Anyway, I expect she felt threatened by you. She was jealous."

"Ooh, I like that idea. Me, a humble small-town psychic, making celebrity psychic Tessa Valentine green with envy. By the way, I figured out how she got into my locked shop."

"Did she use her psychic abilities to unlock the door?"

"No. When I was driving her to the bookstore, she asked if I had any tissues, and I told her to look in the glove compartment. I keep a spare key for Seeing Beyond in there, and Tessa must have grabbed it without me noticing. Danny gave it to me this morning; it was on Tessa when they found her, and now that the case is closed, he said he wasn't afraid to admit they had evidence that made me look bad."

"She must have seen the key and realized she could hide out at your shop," Emily surmised.

"Maybe. Either way, it means she was a thief as well as a fraud."

Sage and Emily had reached the door of Sage's office building, and Emily said in an undertone, "All right, no more fraud talk until Tessa is gone. We don't want her ghost sticking around to pick an argument with you."

"Agreed." Sage led the way upstairs, and soon, she and Emily were seated on the sofa inside Seeing Beyond.

"I'm going rug shopping next week," Sage said, looking at the floor with distaste. "Even though Tessa wasn't a messy corpse, there are still traces of a dead body all over my rug. Yuck."

Emily just snickered in response. Sage was even more squeamish than she was.

Sage's voice shifted into a flat, low tone as she said, "Tessa, I know you're here. Your killer has been caught, and those books you left out at Under the Covers helped! Because of your clues, Emily realized it was your assistant, Vic, who killed you."

Sage leaned toward Emily and whispered, "I'm feeding her ego a bit in the hope it encourages her to leave." She straightened up and returned to the voice she used when communicating with ghosts. "Tessa, your work here is done. Vic has been arrested. You helped us solve your murder. Now, it's time for you to move on. Once you cross over, you can learn how to talk to other psychic mediums. Think how much attention you'll get when you start making guest appearances at séances! This is a whole new opportunity for you."

"You're really selling it," Emily said.

"Tessa, you know from your own work that this isn't the end, and you don't need to be scared of what's next," Sage continued. "Go enjoy your next adventure."

Emily heard a noise from the direction of the bookcase behind Sage's desk. Slowly, a book on one side of the bookcase slid out of its spot and crashed to the floor. The book next to it followed, and the next. The books continued to slide off the shelf, with the movement heading in the direction of the door.

Once the entire row of books had been pushed to the floor, the overhead lights snuffed out.

"Such a diva!" Sage said. She was trying to sound exasperated, but her excitement and pride were shining through the facade. "She flicked the light switch by the door on her way out. Leave it to Tessa to make a dramatic exit like that."

Emily didn't need to ask Sage whether Tessa was gone or not. She could feel her absence, and she leaned back against the sofa with a sigh of satisfaction. "And my final guest from this week is gone. You know, they were supposed to stay with me through Sunday. I now have an entire free weekend ahead of me."

"Good!" Sage enthused. "You've earned a break!"

"I really have." Emily smiled happily. "Scott is at peace, we helped solve two murders, and my psychic medium best friend is back in business. I'm ready to celebrate the wins and get some rest."

"Just remember, it's only temporary rest, not eternal rest."

"Ha, ha."

There was a low moan from the direction of the hallway, and as Emily and Sage rushed to the door, the noise grew to a wail. When Sage opened the door, the noise ceased. The hallway was empty.

"Your rest might be short-lived," Sage said, grinning. "Now that Oak Hill is so full of ghosts, I think we're going to have our hands full helping them."

"Good. I'm ready. Right after I sleep in tomorrow morning and laze around the house all day."

A NOTE FROM THE AUTHOR

As Sage said, Emily has earned a break. Now that Scott's story has been wrapped up, I'm getting ready to launch my new Nightmare, Arizona paranormal cozy mystery series. ***I have included the first chapter of Homicide at the Haunted House for you here, so you can read it right now!***

That doesn't mean the Eternal Rest Bed and Breakfast series has reached "The End," though. There are still a lot of mysteries to be solved in Oak Hill, Georgia! Plus, will Emily be ready for romance soon? And if so, who will she choose? Will Officer Newton ever become a believer? How long will it take Sage to fully recover her mediumship abilities?

As you can see, I still have plenty of Eternal Rest stories to tell! While I'm writing, will you please take the time to leave a review? Reviews mean the world to indie authors like me, because they help new readers find us. Thank you!

Eternally Yours,

Beth

P.S. You can keep up with my latest book news, get fun freebies, and more by signing up for my newsletter at Beth-Dolgner.com!

ABOUT THE AUTHOR

Beth Dolgner writes paranormal fiction and nonfiction. Her interest in things that go bump in the night really took off on a trip to Savannah, Georgia, so it's fitting that her first series—Betty Boo, Ghost Hunter—takes place in that spooky city. Beth also writes paranormal nonfiction, including her first book, *Georgia Spirits and Specters*, which is a collection of Georgia ghost stories.

Beth and her husband, Ed, live in Tucson, Arizona. Their Victorian bungalow is possibly haunted, but it's not nearly as exciting as the ghostly activity at Eternal Rest Bed and Breakfast.

Beth also enjoys giving presentations on Victorian death and mourning traditions as well as Victorian Spiritualism. She has been a volunteer at an historic cemetery, a ghost tour guide, and a paranormal investigator. Beth likes to think of it all as research for her books.

Keep up with Beth and sign up for her newsletter at
BethDolgner.com

BOOKS BY BETH DOLGNER

The Eternal Rest Bed and Breakfast Series

Paranormal Cozy Mystery

Sweet Dreams

Late Checkout

Picture Perfect

Scenic Views

Breakfast Included

Groups Welcome

Quiet Nights

The Nightmare, Arizona Series

Paranormal Cozy Mystery

Homicide at the Haunted House

Drowning at the Diner

Slaying at the Saloon

Murder at the Motel

Poisoning at the Party

Clawing at the Corral

The Betty Boo, Ghost Hunter Series

Paranormal Romance

Ghost of a Threat

Ghost of a Whisper

Ghost of a Memory

Ghost of a Hope

Manifest

Young Adult Steampunk

A Talent for Death

Young Adult Urban Fantasy

Non-Fiction

Georgia Spirits and Specters

Everyday Voodoo

Keep Reading for a Sneak Peek at Beth's Next Series!

WANT MORE?

Book One of the Nightmare, Arizona Paranormal Cozy Mysteries

Murder, Monsters, and a Midlife Crisis in Nightmare, Arizona.

Divorced, broke, and broken down in the old mining town of Nightmare, Arizona, Olivia Kendrick is desperate for a job. At forty-two years old, she never thought she would be starting over like this, let alone in a tucked-away town filled with tourists, offbeat residents, and an outspoken UFO hunter.

Olivia takes a job at a year-round haunted house, but when she arrives for her first day, she faces real horror: a local man's body has been dumped at the front entrance.

Olivia is an immediate suspect. After all, she's a stranger in town. As Olivia tries to find the real killer to clear her name, she begins to realize her co-workers aren't just putting on a show every night at Nightmare Sanctuary Haunted House. And why does the "dog" running around have such long fangs?

Things only get worse when Damien Shackleford, the son of the haunted house's missing owner, shows up. He might be handsome, but his attitude makes everyone miserable. Olivia must forge a new life, solve a murder, and decide who's more of a monster: Damien or the actual monsters she works with…

Keep Reading for a Sneak Peek at Chapter One!

Sneak Peek of Homicide at the Haunted House, Book One of the Nightmare, Arizona Paranormal Cozy Mysteries

CHAPTER ONE

I crested the hill and squinted as the late-afternoon sun glared through my windshield. Ahead of me, the Interstate stretched in a long, straight line for miles before finally disappearing into a cluster of hills, which were slowly darkening to a purple hue on the horizon.

Red dots danced in my vision, and I blinked, willing my eyes to adjust. No, I realized, it wasn't the sun affecting me. I was seeing brake lights, a whole sea of them about a mile ahead. Beyond them, blue lights flashed. I couldn't see what had happened up there, but I knew it wasn't good.

The three cars in front of me dove off onto an exit ramp, and I followed suit. As the Interstate continued down the hill and into the valley, I turned left onto a two-lane road that bridged the Interstate and wound south through the hills. An army of tall Saguaros threw long shadows, and scrubby trees clung desperately to the rocky slopes. Ever since I had crossed the state line into Arizona, the landscape had become increasingly desolate. Everywhere I looked, there was a different kind of cactus waiting to stab me.

I sure hoped the drivers ahead of me knew where they were going. Their cars looked shiny and relatively new, which meant they probably had GPS. My car was so old it only had a radio and a CD player, and I probably hadn't owned any CDs for at least a decade. That meant I had been listening to local radio stations for the past two days and five states. The last time I knew so many top-forty songs, I was in college and a full three dress sizes slimmer.

I didn't even have a cell phone anymore, so I couldn't use the map on that. With that thought, I pressed the gas pedal just a little harder to close the small gap between me and the car ahead. There was no way I was going to risk losing sight of them on this windy road. I needed to be able to find my way back onto the Interstate so I could finish up what had to be the most miserable road trip of my life. Just five more hours, and I would be at my brother's house in San Diego. Even if I stopped for some cheap gas station coffee, I would still make it there before midnight.

There were no crossroads as I continued to follow the other cars south. The road was slowly gaining elevation, but it definitely wasn't curving west at all. We were going farther and farther away from the Interstate.

I had been driving on the road for at least twenty minutes when I saw another blinking light. This time, it wasn't from brake lights or police cars. It was the yellow "check engine" light on my dash.

"Oh, come on," I moaned. My eyes darted across the dash, and I watched as the needle on the engine temperature gauge slowly rotated upward. "No, no, no. Please, no. I need to get to San Diego tonight!"

Here's the thing about talking to your car: it doesn't talk back, and it definitely does not listen.

Finally, I saw a stop sign coming up. The cars ahead of me were all turning right, going west again to parallel the Interstate. When it was my turn at the intersection, I glanced right and saw nothing but more sharp plants and rocks. I looked straight ahead and saw a plywood sign with faded blue paint that read, *Repairs! Oil Changes! A/C Coolant! 3 Miles Ahead!*

I jumped at the sound of honking, and I glanced in my

rearview mirror to see a line of cars snaking behind me, all waiting for their turn to get back to civilization, too. I looked at my dash hopefully, but the engine temperature needle was still winding its way upward, creeping closer to the red "don't you dare keep driving" part of the gauge.

I sighed, switched off my turn signal, and went straight.

"Only three miles, car," I said coaxingly. "You can do this."

It couldn't. I had only gone about a mile and a half when the dash suddenly lit up like a Christmas tree. The temperature needle was buried in the red. I lost count of the expletives I muttered as I guided the car onto the narrow shoulder and turned it off. I was on a steep incline, so I pulled the parking brake and hoped the car would stay put.

Actually, part of me hoped it would catch on fire, roll off the side of the hill, and explode on contact with the rocky valley below, but then I'd really be stranded.

I figured there was no point trying to take any of my belongings with me. The little I had left to call my own would probably be safe out here: I hadn't passed a single car since I had gone straight through that stop sign. I grabbed my purse, locked up the car, and started walking.

As I hoofed it up the incline, I noticed there were fewer cacti but quite a few taller, leafier trees dotting the landscape. It seemed that the higher I climbed into the hills, the less the land was trying to kill me. It wasn't much of a silver lining, but it was all I had.

It was hot out, probably one-hundred degrees or more, but at least the sun was sinking fast. By the time I finally spotted a white-washed cinderblock garage around a curve in the road, the sun had just sunk beneath the hills on the horizon.

The same faded blue paint I had seen on the plywood

sign was also on the side of the garage, with *Done Right Auto Repair* written in a flowing script. By the time I walked through the creaking wooden door at the front of the garage, I was sweaty, tired, and fighting the urge to just start yelling. It wasn't that I was mad at anyone. I was just fed up with the whole situation.

"Be right with you!" The man's voice echoed from a room behind the front office, and soon, the body it belonged to appeared in the doorway. He somehow looked like the garage itself. His oil-streaked white overalls seemed too large on his lean frame, and his blue eyes were as faded as the paint on the sign. He smiled, his teeth bright in contrast to his tanned face. "Good timing. I was just closing up for the weekend. What can I do for you?"

"For the weekend?" I repeated. I brushed a sweaty lock of auburn hair out of my eyes.

"Yeah, I take weekends off so I can spend more time with my daughter." The man gave me a quick wink. "Unless, of course, it's an emergency."

I waved vaguely in the direction I had come from. "My car overheated. I had to ditch it on the side of the road."

The man nodded grimly. "That is an emergency. Let's get your car towed up here, then we'll figure out what's next. I'm Nick Dalton."

"Olivia Kendrick. Thanks." Nick pulled a rag with even more oil and dirt on it than his overalls out of a pocket. He wiped his hand on it before reaching out. I tried to keep my grimace to a minimum as I shook his proffered hand, since I had no interest in being covered in oil, too. Nick's grip was warm and firm, and I was surprised to feel my lips start to turn up into a genuine smile. There was just something comforting about him. *I might be stranded in the middle of nowhere,* I thought, *but at least I'm stranded with this guy.*

In just a few minutes, I was sitting uncomfortably in the

passenger seat of Nick's tow truck. The springs sagged, and a rip in the faux-leather upholstery had been covered up with silver duct tape that squeaked every time I shifted. Nick asked me a steady stream of questions as we drove, like where I was headed to, where I had come from, and how I had managed to stray so far from the Interstate.

When we pulled up next to my car and came to a stop, Nick whistled. "You came all the way from Nashville in that?" He sounded both horrified and impressed.

"It's all I could afford," I said stiffly, shrugging.

Nick looked at me keenly. "I just didn't think someone carrying such an expensive designer purse would drive a hunk of junk like that."

Ouch. I made a mental note that even though Nick looked like a mess, his mind was sharp. I instinctively clutched my purse closer. When I had sold everything off, I had flat-out refused to get rid of my purse. Some things were non-negotiable.

It was nearly dark already, and Nick grabbed a big silver flashlight from a box that sat between the driver and passenger seats. "Let's see what we're dealing with," he said before sliding deftly out of the tow truck.

I got out a lot less gracefully, scrambling my way down. Nick was already opening the hood of my car, though, so at least he hadn't witnessed my awkward exit. I walked over to him, and my eyes followed the beam of his flashlight, which he trained at my radiator. I crossed my arms and tried to look like I understood what I was seeing.

Nick suddenly dropped onto his knees to peer underneath the car. He stood up again, produced that same dirty rag, and pulled the dip stick out of the oil reservoir. I suppressed a sardonic laugh. The last car I'd owned hadn't even had a dip stick for checking oil. The car's computer would simply know if the oil was low and beam a message to the dash to tell me it needed service.

"I hate to say it, but you've got an oil leak," Nick said. To his credit, he actually did sound sorry about giving me such bad news. "I had hoped you just needed to top off your radiator fluid, but it's going to take more than that." Nick turned to me with a sympathetic expression. "Even if I order the parts first thing in the morning, they won't arrive until Monday or Tuesday. We don't have that same-day service like in the big cities."

I bit my lip as I quickly and silently did math in my head. Repairs to the oil system on my car plus at least three nights in a motel was going to add up fast.

Nick seemed to know what I was thinking, because he grinned at me. "Luckily, my parents own a local motel, and they're always happy to give a discount to my customers."

I nodded. My only other choice was to ask if there was a couch at the garage I could crash on.

Nick got my car hooked up to his tow truck, and we made the short drive back to his garage. Once he had unhooked my car, I unloaded my two suitcases of clothes, leaving my few boxes of keepsakes in the trunk. I wouldn't need those in the motel.

The drive to the motel was a cramped one. I had expected Nick to have a normal car, but we climbed into the tow truck again. Nick had managed to wedge one of my suitcases behind the seats, but the other was balanced half on my lap and half on the box between us. Every time we hit a bump, I worried the suitcase would knock into Nick's arm and send us careening off the road.

We only drove about a mile before I started seeing a few houses and side streets. We passed a building with several shops in it, and then we rounded a curve, and I found myself looking at a sleepy little town. I couldn't see much in the dark, but the soft yellow streetlights stretched across a relatively flat space dotted with low buildings.

A neon sign blinked on the left-hand side of the road.

Green letters reading *Cowboy's Rest Motor Lodge* were topped by a yellow cowboy hat. "Here we are," Nick said proudly.

The motel itself looked as mid-century kitsch as the neon sign. It was made of white cinderblock, like the garage, and it had two wings that ran straight back from the street, with parking spaces in between them. At the front of the motel, centered between the driveways that led in and out of the parking area, there was a small, two-story building with neon signs in the front windows that read *Office* and *Satellite TV!*

Nick pulled up right in front of the office. He had already climbed out and unloaded both of my suitcases by the time I had made it out the passenger side. If I was going to be riding around town with him, I would really have to work on my exit skills.

Nick opened the glass front door of the office, ushering me into a room with a thick brown carpet and a front desk made of Formica. The woman behind the counter had a grin that was identical to Nick's, and she spread her plump arms in a welcoming gesture. "Welcome to Nightmare, Arizona!"

Manufactured by Amazon.ca
Bolton, ON